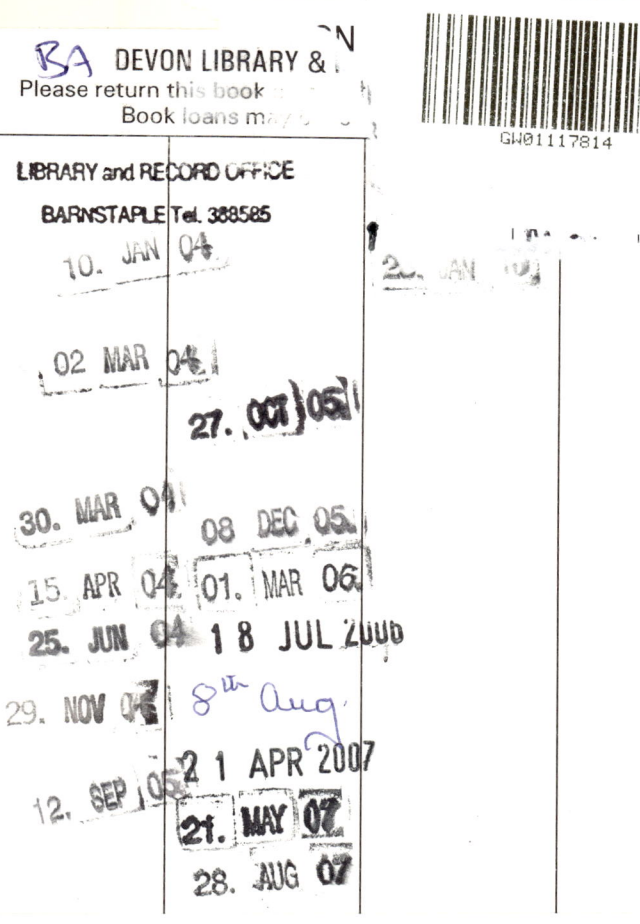

GLASBY, John
Bowie of the Alamo

D10930641 X 0 100

Bowie of the Alamo

Louisiana and Texas in the early rugged days were seething with power-hungry, hard-hitting men. Among these men was James Bowie, adventurer and pioneer. He was a large, fair and outwardly peaceful man, but with a reputation throughout the States for his strength and daring. Moving to Texas, he was well received by the Mexicans there, but for all this, he took part in the revolt against Mexico and was a leader at the battles of Nacogdoches, Conception and the Grass fight.

It was here, on the borders, that he used the long-bladed hunting knife with such a devastating effect. so that it long became one of the favourite weapons there during the early years in the raw, new country far to the south of the United States. Although ill with pneumonia during the final assault at the battle of the Alamo, he shot down several of the attackers from his bed.

This is a blazing novel of the early West and of the men who took part in the final shaping of the country.

Bowie of the Alamo

JOHN GLASBY

A Black Horse Western

ROBERT HALE · LONDON

© 1964, 2002 John Glasby
First hardcover edition 2002
Originally published in paperback as
The Trail Blazers by Chuck Adams

ISBN 0 7090 7214 7

Robert Hale Limited
Clerkenwell House
Clerkenwell Green
London EC1R 0HT

The right of John Glasby to be identified as
author of this work has been asserted by him
in accordance with the Copyright, Design and
Patents Act 1988.

*All characters in this book are fictional,
and any resemblance to persons, living or dead,
is purely coincidental*

Typeset by
Derek Doyle & Associates, Liverpool.
Printed and bound in Great Britain by
Antony Rowe Limited, Wiltshire

1
DEATH AT NIGHT

For several days there had been no trouble. The wind blew straight off the sea and the days were cloudless and warm. Checking the bridle on the tall, black stallion, Jim Bowie began to feel easier in his mind, glancing at the others squatting in the lee of the hill, although he reminded himself that their respite was probably only temporary.

The day had dawned with light mists on the river where it flowed down into the Gulf of Mexico. The sky was a deep blue, except low in the east where pink and purple clouds showed over the land, clouds which generally appeared as though with the purpose of greeting the sun when it rose.

Going back to the others, he sank down on to the rock. Nearby, the horses snickered quietly. Collie Thorpe looked coldly across the narrow stretch of land between the water and themselves, and said: 'You think they'll try to land tonight?'

Bowie nodded. 'They'll come,' he said confidently. He rubbed the back of his hand across his forehead. He was a big man for that part of the country, heavily built, still only in his late teens. He never wore a hat, even in the wet weather, and his crinkly hair came low on the nape of his neck, his eyes dark and sharp.

Thorpe looked out across the river and his eyes glittered brightly. 'How much longer do we have to wait here?'

McGee, the other man, said sourly: 'One of these days, that pirate Lafitte is goin' to get himself caught and strung up from his own yardarm. The Navy is on his trail and they'll get him sooner or later as sure as my name's McGee.'

Collie Thorpe glared at him, but said nothing. Bowie got suddenly to his feet and stared down at the two men. He said softly: 'You don't argue like this when he pays you your share.' He paused, then threw back his head and laughed loudly. 'What have you got to be so puffed up about? We run those black slaves into this country and we get paid well for it.'

'Seems to me we have to run all of the risks and Lafitte gets most of the money. They bring a good price in New Orleans and this French pirate takes the lion's share.'

'Perhaps you'd like to argue that out with him when we meet him,' murmured Bowie softly.

'I'll have it out with him when the time is right,' grunted the other harshly. He slapped at a mosquito and a sudden gleam came into his eyes, then they clouded again. Bowie watched the other closely. These sudden moods of McGee's were quite unpredictable and the other seemed to pull his mind away from his anger with an effort. However, he did not think that the other would try to argue the point with Jean Lafitte; the other did not have that kind of courage. Lafitte was a dangerous man to tangle with. Nobody seemed to know from what strange realms he had come. Quite suddenly, he had appeared on the Louisiana coast south of New Orleans, setting up his headquarters, there, using his pirate ships to bring in contraband and Negro slaves. Soon or later, the Navy would get him, but until then there was no doubting that he was one of the most powerful men along that part of the American coast.

At noon, they moved closer to the coast, seeing no one on the way. This particular stretch of the coast was being closely watched now by men anxious to stamp out the illicit entry of slaves into the country; and in addition, there were other men from New Orleans determined to take the slaves themselves, men who were not averse to fighting even the pirates led by Lafitte if they thought they could lay their hands on some of the Negroes. They, too, would be watching the coast, waiting for the pirate ships to move in during the hours of darkness. That morning, Bowie had killed a deer and they ate well from the hams, a heavy branch thrust through the hock of the deer's leg so that it could be hung over the fire. Since they had made camp in the lee of the hill, there was little chance of the smoke from the fire being seen, particularly with the wind blowing off the sea.

Thorpe took a bottle of rye from his saddlebag and passed it round. When it was empty he tossed it into the brush with a scowl. Chewing on the deer meat, Bowie eyed him anxiously. He had the feeling that the older man was beginning to regret coming into the business with Lafitte and the talk about wanting a bigger cut of the profits was merely an excuse to try to get out of it. As for himself, he was not quite sure how he felt about it. The excitement was the real incentive as far as he was concerned. A woodsman first and foremost, money was of little importance to him. A creature of the great outdoors, he had spent almost the whole of his life in the open since he had been brought to Louisiana at the age of seven from Georgia.

By mid-afternoon, the sky to the east had darkened and the wind had taken on a cold edge with the threat of rain approaching from the south-east. Bowie stood in the centre of the small clearing, with Thorpe's scowling countenance on him, then turned to glance at the top of the hill nearby, the crest hidden in the thick trees which grew there. Moving away to where his horse was hobbled, he said quietly: 'I reckon I'll ride up to the top of the hill and take a look around. I've got a feeling there may be trouble brewing and I always like to know the direction it will come from before it strikes.'

'There'll be rain before the afternoon is out,' said McGee casually.

Bowie nodded, but made no further comment. Swinging up into the saddle, he put his mount to the slope, all of his old caution and training coming to the fore now. This was something he had felt several times in the past, and from previous experience, he knew better than to ignore the sensation. Riding towards the summit was not as easy as he had thought it would be. The tip of a narrow stretch of open ground showed to his right, but he ignored it. Riding over against a bare rock wall, below the rise of the crest, he felt uneasiness riding with him. Climbing still further, he reached a wide ridge and there he reined up. The scene below him was engulfing, but he knew that he would be unable to see all of it, until he had climbed to the very top, into the trees and in front of him, the trail was such that he doubted whether the horse would be able to make its way through the thickly tangled brush and undergrowth.

Dismounting, he swung down to the ground with a hard set to his jaw, stood for a moment, careful of his footing. He climbed gradually, squeezed around a stubbornly growing clump of bitter-brush, with the clawing, wiry roots thrusting up from the ground, then entered the timber, eyes wary. There were other enemies in these parts, apart from two-legged ones and uneasiness moved with him. Ordinarily, he felt quite at home in the brush, but this was a feeling he had had all day, ever since he had woken at sun-up. On top of the hill, the trees grew thickly, hickory and ornamental sassafras, with some maple. It was a good place for deer, because a fire had killed off a lot of the small stuff in several places a few years before and the growth was crowded with small saplings on which deer liked to browse.

There was a trail leading at right angles over the brow of the hill, cutting across his path and he paused to study it closely, looking for sign. To his keen eye it was at once evident that nobody had used it for several days, possibly weeks and a little of the uneasiness faded from his mind. Moving quietly through the trees, he came to the edge of them, parted a thickly tangled bush and peered down the far slope. It was a much more gradual slope than that which he had just climbed, crossing a wide stretch of prairie ground in the distance, perhaps a mile from where he stood. Squatting on his haunches, he sat there with a stolid patience, letting his gaze move over the whole field of seeable view. There was a faint smudge of grey-black smoke far off in the distance, halfway up the slope of a distant hill. Eyes narrowed, he tried to make out more, but from that distance, it was impossible to do so.

The miserly trail spun its way down into the wide valley and then meandered towards the slope from which the smoke lifted into the still air. Here, sheltered by the hills, the wind from the sea seemed to have died away completely. The seconds ticked by. The drizzle was heavier now but he had not noticed it before. Now he did as it plastered his hair close to his scalp, little rivulets trickling down his cheeks, making his forehead greasy.

He squatted there and watched the smoke for half an hour before making his way back down the steep slope to where his horse waited. Mounting up, he rode the rest of the way. Thorpe was lying on the wet ground close to the fire, drinking from a bottle of rye. McGee sat a few yards away, his back and shoulders against a wide rock, whittling on a piece of wood.

Thorpe squinted up at Bowie as he swung down from the saddle and let his horse move away to the plot of grass where it began to browse with the others.

'See anything from up there?' asked Thorpe harshly.

Bowie nodded his head. 'Spotted smoke about a mile away down the far side. Could mean trouble tonight.'

Thorpe mumbled: 'Why? You reckon it might be some of that gang from New Orleans, on the look out for Lafitte?'

Bowie shrugged his broad shoulders. 'Wouldn't be surprised, Collie. They could have seen their chance of making some money for themselves. We don't know how long they've been camped there, waiting for Lafitte to sail in and land those slaves.'

McGee tested the edge of his knife with the ball of his thumb and grinned wickedly. 'Then why are we sitting around here doing nothing? Why not go up there and finish them before they can start any trouble for us? Better do it now than have them jump us tonight, when we may have a lot on our hands.'

'That makes sense,' grunted Thorpe. He got heavily to his feet, nodded his head slowly, ponderously. His hand touched the butt of the pistol thrust almost carelessly in his belt.

'Let's not act hastily,' put in Bowie. He filled a mug with the hot coffee from the can on the fire and sipped the thick liquid slowly. 'Could be there are more of 'em up there than we can handle, even if we do manage to take 'em by surprise.'

'You think we could take 'em more easily tonight, with our hands full with the slaves?'

'No, but tonight we'll have some of Lafitte's men with us.'

Thorpe paused at that, turned the idea over in his mind. Finally, he nodded in agreement, sank down again on to the wet ground. 'So long as we know they're there,' he grunted. He threw a quick glance at the sky, mouth tight, lips pressed together. 'It'll be dark in another three hours or so. No chance of any moon tonight, not with the clouds coming in from that direction.'

Bowie was wakened at dusk by the harsh cackle of a bird in the brush as it killed some smaller animal, pecking it to death. He rolled over and came upright, immediately awake. Collie Thorpe and McGee were already awake, talking in low tones on the opposite side of the fire. He sat for a long moment, listening, straining his senses to pick up every sound that it was possible to hear. He had lived too long in the open not to be able to pick out those sounds which were important, from others, possibly louder and more insistent, which were meaningless and unimportant.

One of the horses snickered softly. Something big and

heavy rustled through the brush on top of the hill, moved off into the distance. He relaxed slowly. He had not meant to fall asleep that afternoon after he had come down from the hilltop, but no harm had been done. The horse cropped the lush green grass. Getting to his feet, he walked forward, stood looking down at the others for a moment, then lifted his head and stared out over the land. The sun, totally hidden by the thick, lowering clouds which scudded across the heavens, must have gone down only a few minutes before. The mist was beginning to rise over the river, a pale curtain that obliterated all details which lay immediately beyond it, yet still allowing him to see everything far in the distance. From their position on the slope of the hill, it was possible to look out over the top of the floating sea of mist into the clearer land beyond it.

The rain had slackened during the late afternoon. His clothing was damp and the ground had a soggy feel underfoot and already, there was a chill coldness in the air which penetrated his clothing.

'You figure they'll be moving inshore soon, down by the creek,' muttered Thorpe. He was looking beyond Bowie, out to sea.

'Not long now,' nodded Bowie. He frowned. Thorpe never seemed to care overmuch what happened to the Negro slaves they brought in from the pirate ships and moved up country to New Orleans where they fetched a good price on the market. Bowie pondered this as they waited for darkness to fall. Thorpe was one of the bloodiest killers in this neck of the woods; a man who held human life in low esteem, but getting these slaves to New Orleans seemed almost like an annoyance as far as he was concerned. Once they reached the city, he liked whisky and women well enough, but even then he seemed content to take them as they came, did not deliberately go after either. A strange man with complicated ways and thoughts, difficult to really understand.

Half an hour later, they kicked dirt on to the fire, saddled up and rode down to the shore. Now, it was completely dark and there was only the soft sound of the water close at hand, pounding on the rocks some distance away.

'You got the lantern?' hissed Thorpe thinly.

McGee, a few feet away, gave a quick nod. Out of the corner of his eye, Bowie noticed the other edge his way forward, holding the heavy lantern in hands that shook a little from the unseasonable cold. Once, the lantern caught the edge of rock with a metallic sound that carried far in the stillness. The sound brought Thorpe whirling on the other.

'Quiet!' he hissed thinly. 'Do you want those others down on our necks like a swarm of renegade Choctaws?'

'They won't come here,' said Bowie confidently. 'They'll work their way down from the far ridge and wait inland for us to move along the Trace. They probably don't even know that we're here, or that they've been spotted.'

'I hope you're right,' growled the other harshly. He moved a few feet away, out on to a flat stretch of ground among the rocks, staring out over the Bay. There was something about Thorpe that sent a little shiver through Bowie's mind. He had known the other for almost four years; an out-and-out killer, dangerous and evil.

Five minutes passed; then ten. Over the Bay there was only darkness, with the lowering clouds hiding any trace of the moon and the drizzle hazing in from the sea. Then, out in that vast mass of blackness, a tiny light flickered briefly.

Collie Thorpe saw it instantly, must have noticed it at the very edge of his vision, for he swung sharply, facing in that direction. 'There's the signal,' he said tightly. 'Bring that lantern, McGee.'

Bowie stood to one side while the other took the lantern and gave the answering signal, flashing the light on and off with the metal shutter. There came the return flickering of the light from the ship out in the Bay, then only darkness. Thorpe lowered the lantern to the rocks, then strode forward to the water's edge, standing with his hands on his hips, head thrust forward a little and cocked slightly to one side as he listened for the faint sound of oars in that stretching darkness. While they were waiting, Bowie kept a sharp and wary eye on the rocks to their right, the direction from which he expected trouble to come if he had read the signs correctly.

There was no indication of movement off in the darkness. In places, where the rocks lifted tall against the sky, just showing as a darker patch of shadow, he could make out the undulating crests of the coastline, but nothing moved there and he became more and more convinced that the other men whose fire he had noticed, would be lying in wait for them along the Trace, hoping to take them unawares.

The faint splash of oars reached his ears a few moments later and he turned all of his attention to the stretch of water in front of him. Thorpe was now standing knee-deep in the water, oblivious of the cold which must have been numbing his feet.

Gradually, the boats materialised out of the darkness, beaching on the narrow stretch of shoreline as Thorpe guided them in. The first man to leap from the leading boat was Lafitte himself. Pirate, privateer, adventurer, he scorned all attempts by the Government to bar him from the coast of Louisiana.

'You are on time as always, *mes amis*,' he greeted them. 'There was no trouble?'

'Bowie spotted smoke this afternoon, away to the east. Could have been hunters, but they may have been others from New Orleans. If they were, they'll be lyin' in wait for us somewhere along the Trace.' Thorpe stepped out of the water and stood beside the Frenchman.

Lafitte nodded slowly. 'You think you can take care of these men – or would you like some of my men to go along with you into New Orleans?'

'Doesn't look too good to me,' grunted McGee, stepping forward. 'Maybe we could do with a little help and some of your men would welcome a stay in New Orleans.'

Lafitte threw back his head and laughed loudly, then slapped the other on the back. 'What you say is true, *mon ami*,' he grinned. If there was any danger in their present position, he gave no outward sign of it, seemed to be absolutely sure of himself, completely at ease. Turning, he watched while some of his men herded the slaves from the boats. There were heavy chains around their legs, keeping them together and in spite of himself, Bowie felt a little twinge of shame as he noticed that there were some women and children among this lot. Some of them would find decent, honest owners, he tried to tell himself; men who would treat them as human beings. But deep down inside, he knew that the majority would be sold to men who cared nothing for the feelings or the well-being of these people, men who would treat them as less than animals.

Soon, all of the Negro slaves were on shore, standing in a huddled group, shivering in the cold wind and the rain that slanted off the sea.

'We'd better get moving,' said Thorpe after a brief pause. 'There's a long way to travel if we're to cover most of it before sun-up. These slaves are goin' to slow us down a heap.'

Lafitte gave a sharp order to his men. They bent, lifted their rifles from the longboats and moved up to the rocks. The hard sound of the chains shattered the stillness as they moved off, through the rocks, and then along the trail that wound over the grassy slope, around the curve of the hill, north in the direction of New Orleans. The three men walked their horses with the rest of the party. The land seemed to be tilted northward, slanting towards the mythical country around the big towns which had sprung up along the great rivers. Most of the way, it was broken and desolate land, but here and there were vast swamps, stretching areas of green deadliness and death, where men were lost once they set foot inside them, where alligators still abounded, waiting still and silent for the unwary, where to be careless was to be dead.

They travelled quickly for the first three miles, through easy country, Bowie acting as the guide, seeming to know every trail and track through the stretches of thick brush which barred the trail. Some day, this would be settled, cultivated country, but that time was still in the far future. Now, it was wilderness, seemingly untouched by man. The roaming bands of Indians who had lived here until a few years before, had made little, if any, impression on the land itself and it was almost impossible to realise that they had ever been there.

Between the chill and the constant changes of gait, no one in the column had any difficulty in staying awake. In fact, shortly after midnight, the effort of locking his jaws against the inclination to let his teeth chatter in his head, set up a soft roaring in his ears and made Bowie feel tired without feeling really sleepy. They stopped at a small seepage spring that came bubbling across the trail, let the three horses crop the salt grass which grew there. The men stood around the spring, tired, but alert. While they remained there, out of sight of anyone not on the trail, Bowie moved to the top of the gentle slope and scanned the trail behind them. Those others he had spotted, wily and crafty, would have found out by now that the slaves had been landed and that they were now on the Trace. They would be moving up at their backs, may have possibly moved off the trail in an attempt to take them by surprise, not knowing that their presence in the area was known to them. Most of his attention was directed to the trail they had just followed, his ears straining to pick out the slightest sound in the distance. He could make out nothing. The silence and the blackness that lay over everything, seemed absolute. It was still chilly here, even away from the sea, and his shoulders had not yet loosened. When they did, he became more drowsy than he had been all day.

Then came a shock. The sharp report of the rifle came from the trees on the other side of the Trace, down by the spring. Crouching down, Bowie slithered back, keeping his head low. More shots sounded and he guessed that it had been a larger party than he had anticipated, following them, waiting for their chance to attack and make off with the slaves.

Reaching the clearing by the spring, Bowie dropped instantly into the long salt grass. The vivid flashes of the guns showed among the trees and the grey horse which belonged to Thorpe showed like a landmark in the darkness at the edge of the clearing. Lafitte and his men were firing back at the hidden attackers from their position by the bank of the narrow stream. Bowie waited for only a moment to ensure that Lafitte and the others were in no immediate danger, then circled around the clearing, making no sound in spite of his massive build. Fireflies winked on and off in the dimness among the trees. He stood in the dark somewhere to the rear of the attacking force, searching the shadows, listening. He could make out nothing in the dense darkness, but the sounds of the shots told him clearly where the men were and he eased his way forward, cat-footed, as silent as any Indian.

A humped shadow lay directly in front of him and he froze for a moment before realising that the man was dead, had been killed by a bullet between the eyes. Bending, he turned the man over, stared down into the unseeing eyes. He did not recognise the man; there were hundreds like him in the back streets of New Orleans and half a dozen similar towns up and down the Mississippi.

He could hear Lafitte and Thorpe yelling harshly in the near distance. The volume of fire increased from the clearing and it was evident that the attackers, whoever they were, had not expected to find such a large force accompanying the slaves along the Trace. There was a sudden movement in the trees, a confused shouting. The men were fleeing, leaving their dead and wounded in the undergrowth. A tall, thickly-built man came blundering forward. He saw Bowie instantly, knew there was no way of escape without fighting for it and came forward with a savage rush, the glint of the long-bladed knife just showing in his right hand. He had a pistol thrust into his belt, but he made no move to reach for it.

Instead, he swung his left hand, the one Bowie had considered to be empty. Too late, the other saw that it was not empty; and although he twisted his head swiftly to one side, the heavy stone caught him a glancing blow on the temple. Lights flashed through his head as he reeled back, his shoulders hitting the trunk of one of the trees, jarring all of the breath from his body. Only his lightning reflexes saved him then. He knew that the other would be a dirty fighter, the man's face, dimly seen, had a brooding, savage look, heavily-boned and forceful, with a strong hint of cruelty. A face, once seen, which would not be readily forgotten. He heard the other's breath gasp through his tightly-clenched teeth as he strove to bring down the knife. Desperately, Bowie forced himself to hold on to his buckling consciousness, knew that he had to throw the other off, or die.

The man was heavy, strong. Savagely, he swung downward with all the force of his right arm, the blade of the knife swooping towards Bowie's chest. With an effort, he caught the other's wrist, pushed up with all of his strength. Sweat began to trickle down his forehead as he struggled with the other. In the dimness, he could make out the white flash of the man's teeth in the shadow of his face, where his lips were thinned back from them with the supreme effort he was making to drive the knife home.

Slowly, as his head cleared from the force of that first unexpected blow, Bowie's superior strength began to tell. Gradually, he thrust the man's wrist back, heard the other curse under his breath as he overbalanced and fell on to his side. The man fell at Bowie's feet. He rolled, his arms locked around Jim's ankles, tried to pull him down where the fight might be more even. Bowie swayed to his knees, struggled to maintain his balance as the other threw all of his weight against him. The big man's fists were like the hooves of a mule as he battered them against Bowie's face, striving to drive him back while he managed to get to his feet. Bowie stumbled back, forced to give ground as the other surged forward, head lowered like a battering ram, driving it with a cruel force into the pit of Bowie's stomach. Only vaguely was he aware of the shouting and crashing in the undergrowth on either side of him. Every sound seemed to reach him through a thick curtain which robbed it of much of its volume. As he fell back, he was aware of the other moving around him. He didn't think that the man still had his knife, he must have dropped it somewhere in the brush during the struggle. But he was still dangerous, knew that this would be a fight to the finish. He swung his foot at Bowie's head, but the other evaded the blow which might have killed him had it landed. Getting to his knees, he swung his body forward and slightly to one side, taking the other completely off his guard. The savage kick missed by inches and before the man could regain his balance, Bowie was on his feet, moving forward swiftly. The man wheeled, moving awkwardly in the tangle of roots and branches. Deliberately, Bowie smashed his clenched fist directly into the other's throat. The man gurgled with pain, stumbled forward and as he fell, Bowie brought both of his fists down on the back of his neck. The man dropped as though pole-axed, fell at Bowie's feet, unmoving. Bending, Bowie felt the limpness in the other's limbs, then straightened up with a grunt and moved forward through the trees into the clearing.

He heard Lafitte laugh as he stepped into the open, saw the Frenchman whirl instinctively, hand dropping towards the pistol thrust into his belt. Then the pirate relaxed as he recognised him.

'We thought you must have been killed, *mon ami*,' he said lightly. He let his hand drop away from the pistol. Moving forward, he turned over one of the bodies on the edge of the clearing with his toe, stared down into the dead man's face for a long moment, then shook his head. 'They make a big mistake,' he murmured finally, turning away. 'They do not think that we travel with you. They fight like women.'

Bowie nodded, but said nothing. Now that they were sure there would be no further attack, the company moved on again. Far off in the darkness, there was the shrill chatter of some bird in the brush and further still, the hoarse cry of an animal, moving along some nocturnal trail. Apart from these sounds, the night was still and thick around them. As they moved through a stretch of canebrake, it began to drizzle, a thin, misting rain that dripped continually from the low clouds, so that they were soaked to the skin, the bitterly cold wind whipping their clothes tightly around their bodies. It was going to be an unpleasant and uncomfortable night for all of them, but no one made any complaint.

It wanted less than an hour to dawn when they finally came within sight of New Orleans. Here, the trail grew wider, easier, and by the time the long, thin streaks of grey were showing on the eastern horizon, they had entered the outskirts of the town. Already, New Orleans was coming awake. As yet, there were few people abroad on the streets, but yellow light showed in several of the windows and their passage had not passed unnoticed.

The authorities in New Orleans frowned on the import of Negro slaves into the town, but as always, money talked and they were prepared to turn a blind eye to these proceedings, particularly as most of the important people in this part of the territory had slaves of their own and were always ready to purchase others, to work the large cotton fields and plantations which had begun to spring up west of the town.

Tethering the horses in front of the livery stable, Bowie and the others followed Lafitte and his men along one of the narrow, winding alleys close to the waterfront. Refuse and rubbish stood piled high and there was the stench of rotting food everywhere. Bowie stared about him, feeling the tightness in his mind. Life in the towns and cities had never appealed to him. The slant-roofed houses on either side of the alley crowded in on him, making him feel trapped.

Thorpe paused in front of one of the houses halfway along the alley, threw a quick glance up and down the quiet street, then rapped sharply on the heavy wooden door with his knuckles. The dull echoes reverberated through the house and a moment later, one of the small windows was pushed open and a head appeared in the opening, peering short-sightedly down at them.

'Who's there?' The quavering voice reached them from the dimness.

'Collie Thorpe.' The other stood back from the door so that the man at the window might see him more clearly. 'We've got more merchandise for you.'

A pause, then: 'I'll be down right away.' The head withdrew and the window was closed with a rattle. Less than half a minute later, Bowie heard the soft shuffle of feet on the other side of the door, a chain rattled and there was the sound of a heavy bolt being withdrawn. Then the door opened and the other stood on one side to let them enter.

'How many this time?' The other stood in the doorway of the room at the back of the house, peering at them all in turn.

'Enough even to satisfy your demands,' said Lafitte softly. He came forward. 'You always told us that we never brought you enough to make it worth the danger of getting them out of New Orleans.'

'There is always danger,' muttered the other in a low, whining tone.

'Listen, Travis,' said Thorpe harshly. 'There were men waiting for us along the Trace tonight. We killed some of 'em but the rest got clear. I suppose you wouldn't know anythin' about 'em?' There was a note of glacial menace in his tone, a look of suspicion in his deep-set eyes.

Travis glanced up quickly. For a second, Bowie felt certain that he saw a flash of fear cross the other's face; but it was gone so quickly, that he could not be sure that he had really seen it.

'There are many men in New Orleans lookin' for a way to make some easy money,' he retorted. 'Why should you think that I had anythin' to do with them?' He let his glance slide away from Thorpe's face to McGee.

'Because you could have figured, in that scheming mind of yours, that perhaps this way, you could get them more cheaply than if we brought them over the Trace. But you didn't figure on us spottin' their smoke during the afternoon, and you didn't know that Lafitte would come with us, bringing some of his men.'

'You speak like a fool,' muttered the other sharply. 'All that concerns me is getting these slaves.' His voice took on the old whining edge as he went on: 'None of you knows of the danger there is, getting them out of the city. The authorities—'

'The authorities in New Orleans are perfectly aware of what is happening under their noses,' said Thorpe swiftly, cutting in on the other. 'These slaves are too important to the big plantation owners for anybody to try to stop the traffic.'

Travis bit his lower lip. There was a crafty look on his thin, pinched features. Then he gave a brief shrug of his bony shoulders. 'Have it your way, Thorpe,' he said thinly. 'Wait here and I'll get the money.'

Travis went through into the other room. Bowie walked over to the window, ignoring the slaves huddled together in one corner of the room. What happened to them now was none of his business, he reflected. They had fulfilled their part of the bargain, and now the rest was up to Travis.

Thorpe said: 'You will be anxious to get back to your ship, Jean.'

Lafitte gave a negligent movement of his head which could have meant anything. 'We can return tonight,' he said lightly. 'There will be no trouble there.'

'You know that there is a price on your head?'

'Of course. But they have to catch me first, and that will not be easy. I know all of the bays and creeks around the American coast – and others further away where they could never find me. The ship will be quite safe.'

Bowie felt a little shiver go through him at the other's

quiet words. The man seemed supremely confident, sure of himself even though he knew that the Navy had ships out looking for him in an effort to stamp out this illegal trade in slaves. Some day, perhaps, if the authorities failed to catch him, the other would sail back into those strange seas from which he had come and nothing more would be heard of him. Already, there was talk that Jean and his brother Pierre had set up some kind of headquarters in the Bayou Barataria on the other side of the river. From there, it would be simple for them to smuggle in more and more slaves from Cuba and the West Indies.

The door opened and Travis came back, looking incongruous in the long white nightshirt which he still wore. Carefully, he divided the coins among them. Bowie saw Collie Thorpe's eyes glow a little with a speculative expression, knew that the other was probably thinking of the rest of the gold which Travis must have hidden away somewhere in the house. But although he looked harmless enough on the surface, there was something about this little man which made Bowie pause and seemed to have the same effect on Thorpe. He gave the impression that although he seemed meek and harmless, he was far from it; a man who knew how to take risks and how to fight for what he had got. It would not be easy taking his money.

'Has there been any trouble in New Orleans?' asked McGee harshly.

'Trouble?' Travis shook his head. 'The only trouble we get these days is when they sell drink to those Choctaws. We've had them running wild through the streets before now and the soldiers seem to be unable to stop 'em.'

Bowie heard that in silence. He had met up with renegade Choctaws before now; knew the kind of savage they were, ready and willing to throw in their lot with any man provided they were paid with rifles and salt.

The fat woman behind the counter in the saloon gave the three of them a queer look as they entered, then reached under the bar and brought out a couple of bottles of rye and three glasses. There had been no welcome on the woman's face and Bowie guessed that she knew who they were and why they were in New Orleans. Even in a city like this, peopled by the lowest dregs of humanity, they still tried to cling to what little pride they had, looking down on men such as themselves. They made their way to one of the tables, sat down with the bottles in front of them. Outside, there were the usual noises of the city coming awake. Unseen hooves thudded along the narrow street and there was the sound of heavy boots clumping on the sidewalks. From somewhere just beyond the doors, there came the sound of a woman's loud peal of laughter, followed closely by the hoarse guffaw of a man.

Even now, he thought, the pirate crews of the Lafittes could walk abroad in the streets of the town without hindrance. He poured liquor into his glass and gulped it down, grimacing as the raw whisky burned the back of his throat. He remembered the unfriendliness they had met from the woman at the bar, knew that it extended throughout the whole of the town. This was the meeting place for all of the gamblers and killers along the whole length of the Mississippi. The people here tolerated the situation only because they had to, because they knew that if they didn't, they had no real force to stop the lawless from taking over completely. Therefore, it was only to be expected that they would choose the lesser of two evils and tolerate these men in their midst.

Thorpe sat drinking steadily, talking out his inner vehemence with angry words. Bowie and McGee let him talk on for a while. There were few other customers in the saloon and those who were there, pointedly occupied tables at the far side of the room, evidently not wishing to tangle with men who had come into town with Jean Lafitte and his men.

Leaning back in his chair, Thorpe yelled: 'Another bottle of rye.'

For a moment, the woman behind the long bar stared across at him and it seemed to Bowie there was an angry retort balanced on her lips. Then she evidently thought better of it, for she clamped her lips tightly together, brought out another bottle, came around the edge of the bar, and carried it to their table. Thorpe tossed a coin on to the table and the woman picked it up, stared down at it for a moment before thrusting it into her pocket and walking back across the room.

Looking across at Bowie, Thorpe said in a voice suddenly low: 'How much longer do you figure we ought to stay in this business, bringing in these slaves for Lafitte, I mean?'

'You know of somethin' better we could do?'

'Sure. They tell me that pretty soon the Americans will want to buy the land to the west of here, that if we can get there now and stake our claims, we could own some of the best country there is.'

Bowie lowered his brows in sudden thought. The land which lay to the west of Louisiana, a state that had only recently been purchased by America, belonged to Spain and Mexico. 'You mean in New Spain – the Tejas country?' he asked finally.

'Where else? Plenty of good pickings for a man across at Nacogdoches. Soon America will move in there too and whether they decide to buy the land or fight for it, I figure the men who move in there first will get all the wealth and power they ever dreamed of.'

'Where did you learn all of this? How can you be so sure that any of it is true?' murmured McGee. 'I've heard that the soldiers down there are hostile towards anyone moving into the territory; and there are Indians too, Apaches and Cheyenne.'

Thorpe snorted in disgust. 'There were Indians like that when we moved into this part of the territory, still are, if you care to go and look for 'em. You ain't scared of no Indians, are you, Jim?'

'No.' Bowie shook his head. The hard liquor had warmed his stomach, but now it was going to his head, making it difficult for him to think things out as clearly as he would have liked.

Bowie of the Alamo

'Good. Then why not tell Lafitte now, while he's still in town? There are plenty of other men who would do this sort of work for him. More'n a score that I could name right now.'

'You reckon he'll mind, having to find other men?' grunted McGee. 'He ain't the sort of man I'd like to cross.'

Thorpe made an ugly face. On the table in front of him, his large, ham-like fist tightened into a hard knot. 'I don't aim to spend the rest of my life workin' the Trace, bringing a handful of Negro slaves up into New Orleans, for the kind of money that Travis is payin',' he retorted swiftly. 'Besides, they reckon that Lafitte has got himself a place out in the Bayou just across on the other bank of the river, where he can work his ships all the way up and laugh at anybody who tries to move in and smoke him out. If there's a grain o' truth in that, he won't need us to bring any slaves up from the Bay.'

McGee looked up sharply at that. His voice was slightly slurred as he said throatily: 'He'll never dare make his headquarters so close to New Orleans.'

'Why not?' demanded the other roughly. 'He's thumbed his nose at them for so long, it must be obvious to everybody that they can't do anythin' to stop him.'

There was no answer to that and McGee fell sullenly silent, drinking steadily until he was completely drunk. Bowie watched him as his eyes began to go together. It had been a long night on the trail, especially after fighting off that attack at the creek and the cold, wet weather had made them more tired than usual.

McGee's head fell forward suddenly on to the table, his arms pillowing it. Thorpe eyed him unblinkingly for a long moment, then lifted the whisky bottle and put it to his lips, scorning the empty glass in front of him. He drank until the liquid trickled down the sides of his mouth and dribbled from his chin, then lowered the bottle and placed it back on to the table, though still with his fingers curled about it as if reluctant to let it go. There was no expression on his face, but a certain hardness, a coldness, had come into his close-set eyes. He flickered a quick glance at Bowie, then thrust the bottle towards him. Bowie shook his head to indicate that he had drunk enough.

'All I need now is somethin' to eat and a place to sleep,' he said harshly. His body still ached from the fight with that man in the brush by the creek, a faint stabbing pain lancing through his chest whenever he sucked in a deep lungful of air. Possibly a cracked rib, he thought tautly, sustained when that man had kicked him. He put the thought out of his mind, scraped back his chair and went over to the bar. The woman eyed him sullenly, waiting for him to speak. Her eyes were cold, lips compressed into a hard line.

'You want more whisky?' she said finally. Her gaze went past him to where McGee lay slumped on the table, head pillowed in his arms. 'Looks to me as if that one has drunk enough.'

Bowie shook his head. He said abruptly: 'I want something to eat and a room.'

For a moment, he thought that she intended to refuse. Then she shrugged her shoulders massively, pointed to the door at the far side of the saloon. 'Through there,' she said shortly. As he moved away, she called: 'What about your friend? The same for him?'

Bowie threw a quick glance at Thorpe, saw that the other had heard for he was nodding his head.

'The same for him,' he replied tightly. He made his way across the saloon, noticed one or two of the men at the tables near the wall lift their heads to give him queer looks, then glance away swiftly as they caught his stare laid on them. Pushing open the door with the flat of his hand, he found himself in a small room with no more than half a dozen tables, each covered with a white cloth. He picked one of them so that he could sit facing the door and sank back gratefully into the chair. The whisky made him feel drowsier than before; a not unpleasant feeling which dulled the painful ache in his chest. A few moments later, Thorpe came in, seated himself in the opposite chair.

The meal, when it came, was better than he had expected and he ate ravenously, aware of how hungry he really was. That deer they had killed on the hillside had provided them with a meal, but it had not been cooked like this. When he had finished, he sat back and built a smoke, watching Thorpe eat. The combination of food and black coffee had acted as a stimulant and he no longer felt as tired as before.

'You goin' to think about my plan to move West?' asked Thorpe after a brief pause. 'I figure it would be easy to hitch ourselves on to a train that was movin' that way, go along with 'em. A lot easier and safer than travellin' alone.' He gave a quick grin. 'Besides, we'd make quicker time down river, through Natchitoches and on to Nocogdoches.'

'I'll think it over,' murmured Bowie. He finished his smoke, got to his feet and moved over to the door. Pausing, he turned: 'Reckon I'll have a talk with Lafitte tonight before he moves out. Could be that he knows somethin' of that country.'

'Could be,' agreed the other heavily, 'But it ain't likely that he'll tell you much about it if he reckons you'll be ridin' out on him to go there.'

Bowie said nothing. Closing the door behind him, he moved over to the bar. The fat woman had been joined by a short, thin-faced man whose eyes seemed to dart everywhere whenever anyone spoke to him, almost as if he were afraid to look a man straight in the face.

'You got a place where I can bed down?' Bowie asked.

The hatchet-faced man shrugged, then jerked his thumb towards the stairway just beyond the end of the bar. 'Up there,' he said harshly. 'Find yourself an empty room.'

Slowly, Bowie climbed the wide stairs, paused for a moment at the top and looked back, down into the saloon. He saw the men clustered around the tables all watching him, saw them turn in confusion when they caught his glance on them. Then the door beyond them opened and Thorpe stepped through, glanced up at him, then walked over to the table where McGee slept noisily with his head on his arms.

He found himself an empty room halfway along the narrow corridor at the top of the stairs, went inside, turned the key in the lock and walked over to the window. It looked out on to a square courtyard at the back of the building. A pile of splintered wooden boards lay in one corner, and a heap of rubbish in another. In the grey light it looked dirty and uninviting and the need for the wide, open stretches of country was strong and insistent within him.

2
TWILIGHT STRIP

The night air was cool and fresh after the stale smoke and noise inside the saloon. Bowie felt glad to get away from the cheap whisky smells and the din. He made his way slowly along the narrow streets to where he knew he would find Lafitte and most of his men. There had been no sign of Collie Thorpe nor McGee at the saloon when he had woken late that afternoon and he guessed that McGee would still be sleeping off the effects of the whisky and that the same thing might also apply to Thorpe, although he wasn't sure about the latter. Thorpe was a strange man. He could give the impression of being drunk and yet his mind was still as sharp and as keen as when he was stone cold sober. As he walked, his mind circled slowly around the new facts he had learned since they had arrived in New Orleans. What puzzled him most was Thorpe's sudden desire to get away from this territory, to move out west into the Tejas country where everything was uncertain and the Spanish and Mexican authorities only welcomed those who were prepared to work and to obey the law. Men as lawless as Thorpe would surely find no place there, unless the other really intended to remain close to the river, where he might be able to rob the families who were, at that moment, moving west into that new country, taking with them every sou that they possessed, most of it in American gold.

The more he turned that possibility over in his mind, the more convinced he became that this was really Thorpe's idea; to throw in his lot with the killers and looters along the river and the Natchez Trace. If that wasn't the case, then try as he would, he couldn't make any sense in what Thorpe proposed. His thoughts kept prodding at the problem, trying to turn it over and find some answer buried somewhere underneath. He was still revolving the events of the past forty-eight hours in his mind when he paused in front of the saloon on the waterfront of the city. The harsh singing and yelling came out to meet him as he thrust open the door and stepped through. The lights were dim in this place, whether by chance or design, he was not sure; but he spotted the Frenchman in one corner, drinking with some of his men. There was a long bar across one side of the room with a chipped and stained mirror behind it on the wall. Towards the front of the room were a couple of gambling tables crowded with players and watchers. At a few of the smaller tables, men sat crouched forward over their cards, their eyes intent and their faces tight and grim, the look all men seemed to get when they gambled. Several hardfaced women moved among the tables, the redness of their rouged cheeks showing clearly in the yellow light, women who watched the games or flirted openly with the men.

Bowie moved among the tables, making his way across to the corner, where Lafitte sat, his eyes bright and alert. Even in a place such as this, Bowie guessed that the other was not fully at ease, knew that trouble could come quickly, unexpectedly, and from any direction. There were men in New Orleans who would be willing to take a chance with their lives, to get the reward that had been offered for the pirate's capture.

Lafitte glanced up as he saw Bowie approaching, then got lithely to his feet, extending his right hand courteously.

'So you found me, *mon ami*,' he said warmly. 'Sit down. Where are your friends? Not with you?'

Bowie drank the glass of whisky that had been placed in front of him slowly and then wiped his lips with the back of his hand. He said softly: 'They're around someplace, I reckon. McGee will be sleeping off the whisky he drank this morning, but where Thorpe is, I don't know.'

'He is a strange man, that one,' murmured the other quietly, his eyes never once leaving Bowie's face. 'Very strange. Sometimes, I find it difficult to know what he is really thinking in that mind of his.'

'Right now, he's thinking of movin' west, away from here – into the Tejas country.'

Lafitte's brows went up a fraction of an inch at that. For a moment, it was clear that he had been taken by surprise at this information, then his lips parted in a smile. 'And what would he do there? Be a farmer? I've heard of this country. The Spanish authorities are willing to let in settlers, provided that they will till the soil and be good citizens. But no one could call Thorpe a good citizen, not by the wildest stretch of the imagination. They will hunt him down and kill him. Does he not know that?'

'Perhaps. But Thorpe is one man I feel sure is afraid of nothing.'

'You may be right.' Lafitte gave a quick nod. 'On the other hand, he may have some other reason for wanting to go there. Many settlers are moving west, with all of their belongings, money, guns and wagons. It will be easy to attack and rob them in the Twilight Strip around Nacognotches.'

Bowie sank back into his chair. So the other thought the same way as he did, he mused. Then that was a very distinct possibility. Thorpe was a killer, through and through. He had that burning desire for gold in his veins that he would do anything to get his hands on it. Gold bought everything out here on the frontier, American or Spanish gold, nobody bothered about the difference.

'What will you do if Thorpe does decide to leave?' Bowie asked presently, eyeing the other closely.

Lafitte smiled easily. 'In what way, *mon ami*? If you mean

will I try to stop him, the answer is no. A man has the right to do as he wishes. Now that I can bring slaves up into the Bayou without hindrance, there will be little need to herd them in by night along the Trace from the coast.' He paused. 'Why do you not go with him? There would be gold for the taking.'

Bowie considered that, then shook his head. 'I may decide to go to the Tejas country,' he answered, 'but not with Thorpe. Bringing the slaves into New Orleans was one thing, but murderin' ordinary folk for their gold is somethin' I draw the line at.'

Lafitte smiled broadly, then clapped him on the shoulder. 'I think I understand you,' he said softly. 'But as for Thorpe, I am not sure. Perhaps, if he is not careful, he will find that he has bitten off more than he can chew, as you would say, if he tries to rob the wagons moving along the river to the west. They will make the journey expecting trouble and they will be ready for it when he does come. A man does not uproot his family, everything he has, to move out into a new country beyond the frontier, without reckoning on meeting with trouble, and making sure that he is prepared for it.'

Bowie turned that thought over in his mind, knew that the other was speaking the truth. These people would travel in large groups for safety, not only from the Indians they knew to inhabit that part of the territory, but from the other killers who would be lying in wait for them along the route.

He grew aware that the Frenchman was watching him closely, speculatively. 'And what about you?' asked Lafitte eventually. 'What do you mean to do? Stay in Louisiana, or go west with Thorpe?'

'I haven't made up my mind yet,' said Bowie, a trifle uneasily. The trouble was that he felt unsettled here, would have preferred to move on into the new territories further to the west, but there seemed to be so many things to be taken into consideration that he felt unsure of himself.

'I have always a place for you,' said the other evenly. He poured himself another drink, held out the bottle to Bowie. 'There are more slaves on Cuba and the other islands, waiting to be brought over here and this is a far easier and safer way of making money than anything that Thorpe may contemplate, believe me.'

Bowie glanced at the other over the rim of his glass. There was something about the other which exuded confidence in the man. He always seemed to know exactly what he wanted to do and he always seemed to be doing it without the slightest possibility of hesitation. If he had hesitated in anything he said or did – but then he didn't. He spoke purposefully, was always ready to meet every situation as it arose, planned carefully ahead so that there might not be any mistakes. It would be easy to follow a man such as this, Bowie decided, even though some of the things he did were undeniably wrong.

The Bayou was like the country that Bowie had known all of his life. In places the water was deep enough for a ship such as Lafitte's to get upriver this far and once in this place, there would be little chance of anyone finding it. It was now three weeks since Thorpe and McGee had ridden out of New Orleans, heading westward along the Trace, in the direction of Natchez and Nacogdoches over the Tejas border. Out there was the Twilight Strip which lay between Natchitoches which lay in Louisiana, manned by United States troops and Nacogdoches in Tejas, filled with Spanish troops. In this hundred-odd miles of Sabine wilderness, the outlaws preyed on any travellers moving through from one state to the other and it was here that Collie Thorpe hoped to link up with men like him.

Meanwhile, in the Bayou, things were moving. Jean and his brother Pierre were still concerned with smuggling contraband of any nature into New Orleans. The situation was ripe for this. For more than a hundred years, the old Camino Real now the Twilight Strip had supported more contraband traffic than legal traffic and that did not lessen now, as most Tejas settlements were far closer to New Orleans than they were to Mexico City.

Inside the Bayou, the air was hot and moist. The cold, unseasonable weather had gone, the sun had come with an increasing warmth, lifting the steaming mist from the swamp, so that it hung curtain-like among the tall trees, where their branches met in a thick mat overhead, stopping the direct sunlight from coming through except in places where it succeeded in filtering through small gaps m the leafy roof, but keeping all of the moist heat in, holding it close to the ground where it hung like something thick and tangible, bringing the sweat boiling from a man's body.

This was wild and untamed country. Bowie could hear the croak of the tree frogs among the bamboos and now and then there would be a louder and more prolonged rustle further in the gloom beyond the thick green fronds. The smell of the water was in the air, a wet, sweet, vegetable smell which permeated everything around him, mingling with the dense greenness until it seemed to be an integral part of it, something which could never be separated from the other sounds and smells of the Bayou.

He drew himself upright as he heard the low croaking grunt of an alligator and let his gaze move swiftly in every direction, until he spotted the ugly, warted snout, just showing above the smooth, unrippled surface of the water. He felt a little shiver pass through him at the sight of it, tried to force the feeling away from his mind. There was a sudden movement on the edge of the small clearing. Jean Lafitte came towards him, moving easily and apparently carelessly through the swamp.

'There's a force of men moving out over the river, heading in this direction,' he said as he came up to Bowie. 'They could be trying to find us here.' He did not seem to be unduly worried by the prospect.

'Do you mean to fight if they come into the Bayou?' It was a superfluous question. Bowie realised that as soon as he spoke. Naturally the other would fight. Men heading in

Bowie of the Alamo

from New Orleans could mean one of two things. They could be interested buyers, willing to purchase anything from guns to slaves. Or they could be armed, uniformed men such as these apparently were, intent on making trouble, hoping to enforce a little law and order in this territory.

Lafitte worked his way forward along the slippery edge of the water, keeping his balance effortlessly. He motioned to Bowie to follow. At the edge of the Bayou, there was an open space, over which it was possible to see the river in the distance. Beyond it, on the far bank, was New Orleans. Bowie looked about him as they reached the open ground, thankful of the fresh air which he drew down into his lungs, filling them as much as possible.

'There, *mon ami*,' murmured the Frenchman. He lifted an arm and pointed. 'You see them?'

The other nodded. It was ridiculously easy to make out the men who came toiling towards them, having crossed the river in a couple of boats, now moored to the nearer bank. 'I see them,' he acknowledged.

Lafitte threw a quick glance up at the sky. There were few clouds and those that were visible, lay close on the horizon beyond New Orleans. The sun was a flaring disc at which it was impossible for a man to look for more than a few seconds and even then, he was blinded for several seconds after he had looked away, unable to make out anything through the dancing green mist that hovered in front of his eyes.

'They are fools,' murmured Lafitte contemptuously, 'thinking that they can come and take us by surprise. They do not understand that from here, I know everything that happens on the river and even beyond it. No man can leave New Orleans and head in this direction without me knowing it within an hour.' He smiled thinly and there was something about the curve of his lips and the look in his narrowed eyes that made Bowie suddenly glad that he was not with those men working their way slowly forward from the direction of the river. It was a look that boded ill for them.

'How long before they get here?' 'he asked after a brief pause.

The other pursed his lips, then answered: 'Less than an hour. But once they get into the swamp, their progress will be very slow. They will not know the secret pathways through the Bayou and when they least expect it, we will take them by surprise. If they decide to surrender, then I may allow them to return to New Orleans, after they have given up their weapons; but on the other hand, if they should decide to fight, then I shall destroy them.'

The way he said it, his tone cold and ruthless, indicated that he did not doubt he could do just that.

Turning silently, Lafitte moved back into the Bayou, Bowie following close on his heels. Gradually, he was beginning to understand the workings of the Frenchman's mind, knew how he would plan his ambush for these unfortunate men.

Although they were desperately trying to make no sound as they advanced, it was possible for Bowie to pick out the movements of the advancing men with ease as they came through the tangle of vines and tough grass. Moistening his lips, he crouched down with the rest of Lafitte's men, feeling the damp ground moving under his feet as he shifted his weight from one foot to the other. The bellowing croak of the tree frogs, disturbed by the men moving along one of the narrow, winding pathways, pinpointed their position as clearly as if Bowie were able to see them through the trees.

He crouched quite still, clutching the rifle in both hands, aware of the heavy weight of the pistol at his belt and the knife thrust into it where he could reach down and pluck it out with a single flick of his fingers. Except for the two men who crouched close to him, it was quite impossible for him to make out where any of the others were hidden, although he knew that there were at least twenty men waiting in ambush for the soldiers.

Three minutes later, there was a loud rustle at the corner of the trail, the sound of a heavy body stumbling in the muddy water, followed by a barely muffled curse. Then the first man stepped into view, stood for a long moment staring about him in the green dimness of the swamp. He looked uneasy, clearly suspected that somewhere along this trail, an ambush had been laid for him, but not sure where it was, and knowing that he had to obey the orders which had been given to him by his superiors in New Orleans. He didn't like the job he had to do and after an awkward pause, during which three more men came into sight around the bend in the trail, he lifted his right arm and motioned the men behind him to move on.

He had barely taken half a dozen paces when Lafitte's voice rang out from the tangle of tree roots and vines on the other side of the trail.

'That is far enough, *mon ami*. One step more and I shall give my men the order to shoot. Throw down your arms and surrender.'

For a second, Bowie had the impression that the officer fully realised he had led his men into a trap, that he meant to do exactly as Lafitte had ordered. Then he threw himself down on the soggy ground, yelling a harsh warning to the rest of his men as he did so. Rolling over, the officer tried to bring up his own weapon, but in his sudden fall, he had dropped on top of it and before his finger could close on the trigger, a shot rang out from the bushes and he suddenly reared up, back twisted into an unnatural position, before falling back with a wild, loud cry. He hit the ground and lay still. The rest of the men, warned by his shout, were already down, rolling into any cover they could find.

Edging forward, Bowie saw one man less than five feet away, getting to his knees in the thick brush, clearly believing that there was only danger on one side of the trail. There was no point in wasting a bullet on a man in that position, kneeling and totally unaware of his danger. Plucking the knife from his belt, he held it for the briefest fraction of a second between his fingers, then threw it easily through the brush. It flashed for a moment, then struck the man beneath the left shoulder blade, burying itself up to the hilt in his back. He toppled forward without so much as a moan, crashing on to his face in the vines.

One of the men crouched beside Bowie gave him a satisfied nod, then crawled forward until he was out of sight. Meanwhile, firing had broken out all along that particular stretch of the trail. Bowie heard the faint hum of a bullet going past his head, pulled himself down swiftly and instinctively into the brush. The long Mills muzzle-loader lay close beside him and he carried a single shot pistol in his belt, but there was no doubt that the knife was the best weapon, the quickest and the most silent in his armoury. Crawling forward, ignoring the faint fluttering in his chest, he reached the man he had killed and pulled the knife from his back, wiping the blade on his sleeve. Another two men rose up from the undergrowth, turned and tried to run, the faint light glinting on their uniforms. One died as Tillier fired, the heavy leaden ball entering the man's chest, the force of the impact knocking him off his feet, spinning him round as he felt, the rifle falling from his nerveless fingers into the swamp. The second man hesitated as his companion died, opened his mouth to yell, then closed it with a snap, slipped on the treacherous ground and fell heavily. Before he could rise, Bowie was on him. He kneed the man in the back, making it impossible for him to straighten up. Before the other could utter a single sound, Bowie's hand struck, driving the knife blade home.

Turning quickly, alert for further trouble, Bowie saw that the rest of the soldiers, those who were still alive, had taken to their heels and were running and stumbling back along the narrow, winding trail through the green depths of the swamp. How many of them would manage to get out of the Bayou alive was a debatable point. A man could lose himself very easily here and once he took one wrong step, once he fell into the water, the alligators would make short work of him.

Breathing heavily, he joined the others as they came out of their hiding place. Lafitte thrust the empty pistol back into his waist band, grinning broadly. 'They did not put up as much of a fight as I expected,' he said softly. 'Without a leader, they are like sheep, they run as soon as one of them flees.'

'Maybe the next time they come, they'll bring more men and more guns with them,' suggested Bowie.

'We will be ready for them no matter how many men they bring. What you do not realise, *mon ami*, is that in this country, we can hold off an army. They cannot come in force. The trails through the Bayou are too narrow for two men to travel side by side and they cannot bring up the big guns or we shall blow them to pieces with the cannon on board the ships.'

Bowie stared at the other for a long moment. He thought that his real admiration for the pirate leader began at that moment. Who but Jean Lafitte would have thought of bringing his ships up-river to this point and using the heavy guns on board to repel any attempt to capture him. Leaving the dead where they had fallen, they made their way back to the camp in the depths of the swamp. The smell of roasting meat hung appetisingly on the air as they approached as men turned the hams over the long fires which had been lit in the wide clearing.

'Are you not glad that you decided to remain here with me, and not go off with those two others?' asked Lafitte, looking across at Bowie as they sat down on the warm, moist ground by the fires. 'Here, we are safe from everyone. We can thumb our noses at the authorities, no matter whether they are French, American or Spanish. This is our kingdom where we rule without fear. What more could a man want? All the food he can eat for the asking. Plenty of money whenever we smuggle our contraband into the country, slaves for the taking.'

'And you think that this state of affairs can go on for ever?' Bowie shook his head slowly, positively. 'It can't last. Sooner or later, they're goin' to get around to the idea of driving us out of here. Maybe not this year, or the next, while they have other things to worry them. But it will come, believe me. Time won't stand still for us. They'll try to bring law and order into the country and even if they don't succeed the first time, or the second, they'll come again until they have wiped us all out.'

'So you're still thinking about that country to the west – Tejas?' queried the other. 'Things are even worse there, more unsettled. There are too many cut-throats and renegade white men, not to mention the Indians, for any man to stay alive for very long.'

'Once they've settled any claims to the country, things should sort themselves out. They say that the United States will buy Tejas, as they did Louisiana, so that they have a stretch of the country clear to California.'

'Those are nothing but dreams in the minds of politicians and crooks,' said the other, speaking slowly. He stared into the fire, seemingly lost in thought. Finally, he lifted his head. 'I prefer to remain where things are surer, where a man knows from which direction danger will come and can prepare to meet it.'

'And you think that this is such a place?'

The Frenchman shrugged. 'It's as good as any. I've sailed this coast for almost ten years now. I reckon I know every inlet and creek there is and they have not caught me yet.'

'Maybe that's because they've had more things to do with their troops and ships. Once things are stabilised here, they may find more men and ships and guns with which to hunt you down.'

The thought of leaving New Orleans, of leaving Louisiana and moving west into the Tejas country stayed with Bowie during the whole of that autumn and winter, a thought growing stronger the more he considered it, until when the spring came to the territory and the cold, bitter winds gave way to warmer skies and longer days, he decided to move out. Surprisingly, Lafitte showed no sign of astonishment when he informed him of his decision. It was as if the other had been expecting it.

'How do you think you'll get there, *mon ami?*' asked the other quietly, his face serious. 'A man riding the Trace alone will be dead long before he gets to Nacogdoches. The outlaws along the Trace will kill him just for his horse. There are more than a hundred miles of Sabine wilderness to cross out there before you reach Tejas. Even when you do get there, do you think the Spanish and Mexican authorities will let you stay? I've heard that a man has to be prepared to work hard, to cause no trouble, to pay taxes not only to the Government, but to the Church.'

'All my life, I've lived in country like that,' nodded Bowie. 'I'll make out all right.'

The other studied him for a moment, then nodded his head slowly and grasped his hand. 'I shall be sorry to see you go, Jim,' he said quietly, genuinely. 'But perhaps you are right to go out into this new country. I am a privateer, you are a pioneer. This country will need men such as you if it is ever to be great.' He nodded. 'Better link up with one of the wagon trains moving west. That way, you should escape the attentions of the outlaws who infest that part of the Trace.'

The sun shone warm and bright as Bowie made his way through the main streets of New Orleans. It was late afternoon and the heat head still held its piled-up intensity, the street dusty underfoot. A band of horsemen rode through, kicking up the choking, yellow dust; hardfaced men bent on some business of their own. New Orleans was the great business point on the wide Mississippi. It was a strange river, the Mississippi, the banks of which had become built up higher than the land with the great Bayou on one side, a swamp full of tiny channels and islands that stretched clear to the Gulf of Mexico. No wonder that Lafitte had chosen the Bayou for his hideout. Very few men knew that great swamp and fewer still would dare to penetrate it in search of the pirates.

But at the moment, the Mississippi meant little to Bowie. Somewhere on the western outskirts of New Orleans, he expected to find the wagon trains which, almost every week, left this part of the country and headed west through several hundred miles of wilderness, filled with coyotes and jackals, and men with the habits of both, seeking a new land in Tejas where there was land for the buying, land sold on the basis of families. Some men were keen to set up an empire there, ready to swear allegiance to the Spanish King, to embrace the Catholic faith so that they might become a part of this new land.

On a stretch of ground half a mile from the western outskirts of New Orleans, he came upon the group of heavy wagons, not yet hitched to their teams, indicating that they were not quite ready to move out westward. He let his eyes roam over the men and women seated around them. A couple of dogs ran forward, snapping at the heels of his horse so that he had difficulty in keeping it under control.

A harsh voice yelled something sharply from the nearest wagon and the dogs ran off with their tails curled between their hind legs. Bowie reined his mount and glanced round sharply. A tall, blackbearded man lowered himself from the tongue of the wagon and strode purposefully forward, stood a few feet away with his hands rested, hardknuckled, on his hips, looking up at him. There was both suspicion and hostility in his eyes and clearly visible in the set of his mouth.

'You lookin' for somebody, mister?' he asked harshly.

'Heard you might be considerin' moving out to Tejas,' said Bowie evenly. 'Figured you might not have any objections to an extra passenger.'

The other eyed him up and down closely, still suspicious. Inwardly, Bowie could understand the other's hostility. There would have been several cases in the past of men joining these wagon trains, ostensibly as passengers, but in reality men in league with the pirates and outlaws along the Trace, shooting men in the back whenever the outlaw bands launched their attack.

'You heard right about us moving west, mister,' nodded the other, a hard expression on his bluff features, 'but we don't aim to take any strangers when we move out. How do I know that you ain't working for Lafitte or another of these outlaws?'

'You don't.' Bowie answered quietly, giving no indication of anger at what the other suggested. 'But I do know this country that you'll be moving through and I could help as guide for you. I doubt if any of you will have travelled this way before.' As he spoke, he let his gaze wander meaningly over the rest of the wagons, noticing the women and children particularly, who watched him curiously. The wagons were big, as he had expected, with wooden tubs, axes and large leather buckets hanging along their sides. Most of them would apparently be drawn by oxen, but at least two of them would have horses in the traces. Quite clearly, these people had pulled up their roots from wherever it was that they had previously lived and were carrying everything they possessed with them. There would be good pickings here for any of the outlaws along the Trace and for a moment, he pondered the wisdom of attaching himself to them, knowing that perhaps, if he went on by himself, he might take one of the lesser known trails and slip through the outlaw gangs, unseen, whereas these people would call down every roughneck in the country on their necks.

The big man rubbed his chin thoughtfully. There was certainly nothing about Bowie to suggest that he was an outlaw. He looked exactly what he was – a frontiersman, a woodsman, and there was something about him that suggested a latent strength and reliability.

Finally, the other gave a brief nod, with little of welcome in it, but with some measure of acceptance. 'All right, stranger. Better light and get some food. Hope you ain't got no objection to sleepin' out, but these wagons are all full to the sides, even if we sleep tight.'

'No objection to that,' declared Bowie easily, as he swung down from the saddle. He led the horse forward, following the other to the wagon nearby. 'When do you aim on pullin' out?'

'Day after tomorrow,' said the other. He paused in front of the wagon. 'The name's Henson, Matt Henson. This is my wife Victoria and my sons, Seth and Jacob.' He inclined his head towards the interior of the wagon. 'The other wagons belong to other families who joined us a few days ago. We're all mighty anxious to get to where we're goin', but nobody seems to know much of conditions on the other side of the border, beyond Natchitoches. Some reckon that the United States will buy Tejas from Spain and make it part of this country as they did with Louisiana. Others figure that Spain doesn't intend to sell no matter what the price. But everybody seems to think that there's plenty of land there for settlers, if they're prepared to work it, and keep themselves out of trouble.'

'That's true, I guess,' Bowie nodded. 'But there's a long way to go, over the Sabine, along the Camino Real and that place is the ideal breeding ground for outlaws. Out there, every man makes his own law and uses every means he has to keep it.'

'We're ready to meet trouble if it comes,' said the other grimly. 'We aren't exactly unarmed. Every man here can use a gun and most of the women besides.'

Bowie nodded. He wondered if any of these people really knew what they were riding into, if they had paused to consider the danger that would face them once they left the area around New Orleans and headed out into that terrible wilderness. It was quite apparent that many of them had not. They had been taken in by the thought that there was a new land waiting for them to the west, a place where it was always summer, and they would be free of the restrictions which prevailed here.

He hobbled his mount and went over to the fire that was burning a few yards from the wagon. Squatting beside it, he took the mug of hot coffee which Seth Henson handed to him. Seth was a boy in his early teens, possibly fourteen or fifteen years old, tall and big-boned like his father, with the same open, bluff features. He sat down opposite Bowie, waited while the other had sipped the scalding hot liquid, then asked excitedly:

'They tell me that you've ridden this country before, Mister Bowie. Are there Indians where we'll be heading?'

Bowie grinned. 'Sure, son. Indians and outlaws. Most of the Apache and the Choctaws are friendly and they won't bother the wagon train when we move through, but I can't say the same about the outlaws. They know that a train like this will have plenty of gold on board, maybe rifles. Sometimes, they'll even attack a solitary rider just to take his horse. That's why so few of the smaller wagon trains manage to get through without any trouble.'

The boy's eyes were shining and he thrust a piece of stick into the fire, waited until the end had caught, then withdrew it, held it in front of him, staring at the burning tip. 'My father says there won't be any trouble if we all stick together and take care who joins the train.'

'He could be right.' Bowie finished the coffee, set the mug down. 'It doesn't do to trust anybody out here.'

Matt Henson walked over from the wagon, stood close to the fire, staring round at the rest of the train.

Bowie glanced up at him. 'Do you know where to go in Tejas when you get there?'

The other straightened up, hesitated, then nodded slowly. 'We go to Natchitoches and then on to Nacogdoches. When we get there we see the Governor or Viceroy, whoever he may be. He'll give us further instructions.'

'Haven't you considered the possibility that there may be trouble in Tejas before very long?'

'What sort of trouble?' demanded the other belligerently.

'Fighting, maybe even war. Sooner or later, America is going to want the whole of Tejas to gain access to the countries even further west and if Spain won't agree to sell that country, then there may be war.'

'But that would be foolish. After all, Tejas is ruled from

Mexico City and not only the Spanish soldiers, but the Mexicans will fight for Tejas against the United States. No, my friend, I cannot see the possibility of war breaking out over Tejas.'

Bowie pursed his lips but said nothing. Inwardly, he wasn't quite as sure as the other evidently was. The possibility of war had troubled him for some time and he had wondered just how it would affect him if he were there when war broke out. In the past, he had always been on good relations with the Spanish, but now that he had taken time to look at this problem objectively, it came to him that if it came to the showdown, he would have to fight with the American forces against the Spaniards and Mexicans.

Two days later, in the early morning, almost before the sun was up, they moved out from the narrow valley and began the long journey west. Henson was in the lead wagon and Bowie rode alongside, feeling a strange sense of exultation in his mind. The air was clean and fresh and it was possible to see for miles in every direction as they topped a low rise, then began to move down the far side. The oxen bawled loudly in protest as they strained against the traces and the chains gave off loud, explosive cracks like pistol shots in the still air. The white canvas on the wagons swayed and billowed as they moved. At first, progress was slow, the oxen and horses finding their own pace as the ground grew rougher. They crossed a shallow creek, splashing through the foot-deep water, clambering up the far bank, the wagons creaking ominously, wheels bouncing over the rocks that littered the trail.

Beyond the ridge that skirted the creek, the land grew more open, with long stretches of rough grassland, dotted here and there by clumps of maple and pine. Here, the trail was easily followed. Countless wagon trains had already pulled out this way, leaving their mark on the country. The trail made it easy for them to ensure they kept moving in the right direction; it also made it easy for

Bowie of the Alamo 47

the outlaw bands to keep a sharp eye open for wagon trains.

That night, they camped on high ground some thirty miles from their starting point. The sky had remained clear during the whole of the day and the dust had hung thickly in the still air, dust churned up by the hooves of the horses and oxen, and the churning wheels of the wagons. Those at the rear of the line got the worst of it, and everyone was glad when the order was given to make camp.

It meant that they could get down and stretch their legs, could wash the choking dust from their mouths and throats, turn the wagons into a ring and light the fire in the centre, with the children whooping and playing at Indians around the outside of the circle. There was a small stream less than a hundred yards from the camp site, providing them with all of the fresh water they needed. They had some stock with them and Bowie foresaw trouble unless they were able to keep the small herd together. He broached the subject with Henson as they sat around the blazing fire after dark. There were scattered groups of people around two other fires which had been built from dry brushwood collected from among the pines.

'How do you aim to get this herd all the way through the Twilight Strip?' he asked quietly. 'I've been watchin' it during the day and it seems to me that you'll have trouble tryin' to keep 'em together all the way.'

'We'll make out,' muttered the other thickly. 'You didn't think we'd leave 'em behind, did you? We'll need some stock to start with when we get to Tejas. They tell me that it'll raise more cattle to the acre than any other country in the world.'

Bowie raised his brows a little, lips pressed tightly together. 'Maybe you're right there, but it won't help if you lose 'em all on the way. This is rough country we have to go through and cattle will slow us down. Better take my advice and get rid of 'em in Natchez. There's a hard pull over to Nacogdoches.'

The other turned that over in his mind, then shook his

head with a stubborn set to his chin. 'No. We take them all with us,' he said harshly. 'We brought cattle out with us from the east when we moved into the land around New Orleans and I reckon we know how to handle 'em along the trail.'

'Suit yourself. I'm only tryin' to be helpful. If you are meaning to take 'em all the way, I reckon it wouldn't hurt to get 'em corn fed at Natchez.'

'That makes sense,' agreed the other tightly. He took out a pipe and began to push the brown strands of tobacco into it with his thick fingers. Thrusting a stick into the fire, he applied the burning end to the bowl of the pipe and sucked hard on it until it was going well, then sat back on his haunches, puffing on the pipe.

'Another thing.' Bowie looked hard at the other and lowered his voice. 'When we do get to Natchez, I'd keep my mouth shut about any gold you might be carryin' on the train and tell the other families to do the same. There are plenty of outlaws just waitin' to take it all away from you and murder you at the same time and these things have a way of leakin' out.'

Henson narrowed his eyes, took the pipe from his mouth and studied the glowing bowl closely as if expecting to find the answer to a lot of questions that were haunting him there. Something seemed poised on the tip of his tongue, but he shook his head a moment later, said: 'I don't aim to do any talkin', Mister Bowie. Not to you or anybody else.'

'I see that you still don't trust me.' Bowie grinned a little.

'That's right. No offence to you, but like you told Seth this morning, it ain't wise to trust anybody.'

Bowie was silent for a moment. 'You know,' he began quietly, 'I've been thinking and it seems to me we'd make Natchitoches if we head due west. It's goin' to be a long, roundabout route goin' through Natchez.'

'We heard that the trail north to Natchez and then west was the only one we could take.'

'That's what I figured.' Bowie shook his head. 'But there is a trail due west. It'll cut more'n three hundred miles off your journey.'

'You reckon it's safe?' The other sounded dubious. 'There are violent and lawless men in that country, maybe more than we could handle.'

'I don't see it that way. Sure there are outlaws all the way from here clear into Tejas, but they'll be watchin' the trail from Natchez, not lookin' for a wagon train moving across the wilderness. I figure that we'll see nothin' of outlaws until we leave Natchitoches and head out for Nacogdoches.'

He could see that the other was unsure of himself now, that the idea appealed to him, but there was still that feeling in the other's mind that perhaps Bowie was working hand in hand with the outlaws who infested these trails, that he was deliberately steering them into trouble. It was evidently a tremendous responsibility that the other carried on his shoulders, namely the safety of the entire wagon train and every man, woman and child in it. Any decisions he made, would not be made lightly. On the other hand, the chance to cut off more than three hundred miles and also to take a trail which had not been blazed by other trains moving west, tended to sway him away from the path of natural caution.

'I'll talk it over with the others in the morning,' said Henson firmly. 'It may be that we'll decide to do as you suggest. If we do, can we be sure that you know this country we'll have to cross?'

'I can lead you to Natchitoches and get you there safely,' Bowie declared.

Henson sat quite still for several minutes, staring into the flames, smoking the long-stemmed pipe. Finally, he knocked out the last of the tobacco on the heel of his foot and got heavily to his feet, moving towards the nearby wagon. 'I'll let you know of our decision before we're ready to move out,' he said.

Bowie sat near the fire, watching the other climb on to

the tongue of the wagon, then move into the rear of the wagon. Henson was a strange man, the sort of man this country needed; careful and conscientious, ready and willing to adapt to change. He was not the kind of man to take chances lightly, but would do so when the occasion demanded.

How long he sat beside the fire, it was impossible to tell. The night air held a slight chill as he got to his feet and moved over beside one of the wagons, spreading out his blanket on the ground. Stretching himself out, he pulled the blanket up to his chin and lay on his back, staring up at the sky over his head. The air here was crystal clear, the stars so bright that he might almost reach up and touch them with his hand; constellations marching grandly from one horizon to the other. The camp was still now. A horse snickered from somewhere close by, but that was the only sound. How many more nights would there be like this on the trail? Although he had tried to sound convincing when he had attempted to persuade Henson to turn west instead of heading for Natchez, he was not quite as certain of this as he had tried to appear. There were several hundred miles of bad country to cross before they reached Natchitoches, but fortunately it had been a dry spring and the rivers would be down. They would not have the added danger of putting the wagons across rivers in flood.

Lying there, he thought about the old days, before he had moved into Louisiana. He had only been a boy then and the pictures which formed in his mind were hazy and dim. So much seemed to have happened since those far-off days, so many events crowding into his mind, that it was difficult to fix on any one thing and try to concentrate, to bring it into focus in his mind. Since his parents had died, he had led a lonely, wandering life searching for something, but not sure within his own mind what it was. Somehow, he had the feeling, stronger than a premonition, that he would never find it, no matter where he travelled.

Maybe these people were more fortunate than he was.

They knew, deep down inside, what they were looking for, and they had given up everything they had so that they might have a chance of finding it. There was little content for a man who knew only the long, open trails of the wild, new country; a man who could look after himself could live off the country; a self-contained man, but not a truly satisfied one.

He rolled over on to his side, staring towards the fire a few yards away.

The flames, which had been dying down a little, suddenly caught on the fresh wood that had been piled on top of the fire. Flames licked along the dry branches, blazed as they touched the sap in the dry pine wood. A cascade of red sparks lifted into the still air, hung for several moments over the camp before winking out like a host of fireflies.

Lying there, the thought of McGee and Collie Thorpe popped into his mind, came into his brain suddenly and unexpectedly. Now why was he thinking about those two at that moment? he wondered idly. They had left for the Natchez Trace some months before and he had thought little of them in all that time. Now, when his mind had been turning over a host of other things, he suddenly found himself thinking of them. Perhaps they hadn't turned north for Natchez? Maybe they had cut west in the same direction he had tried to persuade Henson to go. If that was the case, and they were somewhere along the trail, they would certainly not pass up the chance of attacking this wagon train and if they had joined up with other outlaws in this area, then they would definitely have their spies out along the trail, maybe even as far east as New Orleans. That was the logical place for outlaw spies to be, watching for the wagon trains as they built up, then pulled out in large groups, believing that safety lay in numbers, provided every man who travelled with them was a man similar to themselves, men of farming stock, pioneers, heading for Tejas and the new country which belonged to Spain.

He lay quite still on the hard ground, finding no discomfort there. This was the life he was used to, the ground his bed, the stars his ceiling. One of the horses moved restlessly close by and his mind jerked instantly awake. He lifted his head swiftly and peered off into the darkness that lay beyond the ring of firelight, but he could make out nothing. The sound was not repeated and a few moments later, he sank back and fell asleep almost immediately.

3
BORDER TRAIL

'We've talked over the suggestion you made last night, Mister Bowie.' Henson stood with his legs braced well apart as Bowie folded his blankets and placed the bedroll on the saddle. 'We figure that maybe you're right when you say the outlaws will be watching that other trail to the north, the trail out of Natchez. We've agreed to fall in with your plan and head due west, straight for the border.'

'Now I reckon you've all made a wise decision,' said Bowie heartily. He turned back and looked around the circle of wagons, standing out in silhouette against the pale dawn light which was streaking the eastern horizon. Most everyone was up; they rose early on the trail, anxious to move on before the full heat of the day made driving not only uncomfortable, but dangerous, the dry dust getting into the folds of the skin, working its way under the lids of the eyes and this, combined with the powerful, almost unbearable glare of the sun, made it difficult and dangerous to follow the twisting, winding trail.

Henson threw a quick, all-embracing glance at the sky. 'Reckon we'll eat and then move on out,' he said loudly, his voice carrying to everyone in the train.

Less than an hour later, the wagons rumbled off the main trail that began to wind north at that point. Swaying and shuddering, they moved over the rough, stony ground, wheels creaking and jarring. The oxen strained as they hauled the heavy wagons forward. Seated in the saddle, Bowie rode a little way ahead of the train, scouting the ground. Leaving the trail, he swung his head, looking for a high spot not too far from the trail. There was a densely wooded hassock about two miles to the south and a little off the route which the wagons would take. He made for it and didn't draw rein until he had to; when the bay was sweat-lathered and breathing harshly. Without pausing, Bowie sent it angling up the side of the hill. From the trees at the top, he was able to look out over the flat plain that lay beyond. Almost as far as the eye could see, there was only wasteland where very little grew and off in the distance, he thought he could detect the dark shadow of lava beds. The glance he raked the land with was cold and far-seeing. Nothing stirred and it was as if man had never been to this place, as if it stood now exactly as it had when it was born countless ages before.

He sat tall in the saddle for a long moment. The sun laid a wide swathe of yellow light over the land, but was still chilly in spite of the light and his shoulders were slow to loosen. When they did, there was a dull ache suffused throughout his body and to offset it, he built a smoke and lit it, drawing the smoke down into his lungs. It made it possible for him to relax a little. Behind him, the wagon train moved forward with a snail-like pace.

He pinched up his eyes in thought and tried to guess where any outlaws might make their camp if they were watching this trail. It was a terribly long distance that he could see, clear to the lava beds on the horizon and as far as he could see, there was no place for anyone to hide. The thought made him stand a little in the stirrups, but now that the sun had come out, was lifting up from the dead flatness of the horizon, the land ahead was dead and dazzling, with the bush clumps growing less frequent to the west. He scanned every foot of it for an eminence, for a ridge where men might fire down on the plain. There was none. This was flat land, country that had been storm-battered, had had all of the moisture sucked from the arid soil by the hot sun and the drying winds which swept over it, gullied land where every mile looked the same as any other.

It was not going to be easy land to cross with the wagons. The distances were deceptive, the horizons treacherous, a land designed by God to swallow up men and animals, limitless acres of silence and little water.

Wheeling his mount, he rode back down the steep slope. In places, the going was so treacherous that only his weight in the saddle prevented his mount from sliding out of control as stones and boulders bounced ahead of them. He joined the train twenty minutes later, reining his mount beside the lead wagon.

Henson looked at him out of the corner of his eye. 'See anything from up there?' he asked.

'Not much. Bad country, but we've got plenty of water to take us across. No trouble there. It's flat terrain, too, which means we can't easily be taken by surprise.'

Henson nodded his head ponderously. He held the thick leather reins tightly in his huge hands, the hairs on the back of his wrists glistening in the strong sunlight. He set his teeth tight in his head, jaw thrust forward. They rumbled forward around the lee of the hill Bowie had climbed and pushed on into the bare and inhospitable country that lay beyond. Now the sun was getting really hot, heat refracted back from the arid land on either side of their trail. The land changed its character as they drove west, became greyer, more thickly spread with the drifting alkali dust. The animals lowed protestingly as they plodded forward with heads lowered to the earth, their hooves churning up more dust. The land around them looked the same no matter in which direction they peered. It never changed and Bowie had the unshakable impression that it never would, that men could never change this country. It was too big, too wild and untamable.

Then, far off on the horizon, the ground began to rise steeply. The hills became clearer through the shimmering heat as the afternoon progressed, lifting boldly from the dusty plain.

'How far do you reckon the hills are?' asked Henson gruffly, pointing. Thick-necked and low-jowled under the black beard, he sat heavily on the wooden tongue of the lead wagon, his eyes staring a little, protruding from his head as he tried to force his vision through the cloud of dust that swirled endlessly about the slow-moving train.

'Too far to reach by nightfall,' Bowie answered confidently. He studied the terrain that lay between them and the hills. 'Could be the best part of forty miles away; difficult to be sure out here. We'll be lucky if we reach 'em by tomorrow night.'

Henson did not argue. His eyes narrowed a little, then he nodded, glancing about him at the ground nearer at hand. 'Where do you figure we should make camp?'

'I'll scout ahead for water,' Bowie told him. 'Should be a stream less than a couple of miles ahead.' Pulling sharply on the reins, he turned his horse's head and put it into a swift run away from the train. As he rode, the bushes grew more frequent – a good sign, indicating that he was fast approaching moister ground – and topping a low rise, he felt his mount respond under him, quickening its pace, knew that it had scented water. He came upon it less than ten minutes later, a seepage spring that smelled sulphurous, but it was wet and drinkable. Out here, in this desert stretch of country, beggars could not afford to be choosers.

He let his horse drink, paused there for a moment, then turned and rode back to the wagons.

After they had made camp and darkness had fallen over the countryside, Bowie got to his feet and made the rounds of the wagons, checking everything. They were now far enough out from New Orleans for trouble to strike and it was essential to ensure that they were ready to meet it, did not leave anything to chance. Too many wagon trains had been looted, robbed and burned because no one took the sensible precautions of making certain that someone who could be trusted to stay awake, remained on guard through the night, ready to give the alarm if there was an attack.

Finally, he was satisfied, and went back to one of the three wood fires that had been kindled in the circular space between the wagons. There was the smell of hot coffee and sizzling beef. Bowie nodded to the other men near the fire and lowered himself gratefully to the ground, stretching out his legs in front of him. The long day's ride, coming after so long in the Bayou with Lafitte, had told on him and he knew that he would have to get himself hardened to this trail life quickly.

Fallon, one of the other men, handed him a mug of the brew that passed for coffee, muttering: 'Here, Bowie, drink it if you can. Don't seem to matter how you make it, this stuff never tastes as good as that you get in New Orleans.'

Bowie accepted the mug, sipped the hot liquid warily. It went down his throat and brought an expanding warmth into his stomach. True the taste was not like that one bought in New Orleans, but it was wet and satisfying after a long day on the trail. He tore a strip of the hot beef with his strong teeth and chewed on it reflectively for several moments before swallowing it.

'Seems to me you're a little jumpy tonight,' said Fallon, eyeing Bowie obliquely from close by. 'Noticed that you were making the rounds. Expectin' trouble during the night?'

'Not necessarily. But we're quite a way from New Orleans now and this is outlaw country, even though the chances of meeting up with 'em are less than along the Natchez Trace.'

'You ain't suggested anythin' like this before now,' said the other sharply.

'There's been no need to. Ain't likely that anybody would be fool enough to try to attack us within a day's march of the city. But from now on, until we reach Natchitoches, we'll have to have at least one guard watching through the night after we've made camp.'

There was a murmur of voices from the others. Then there came a movement at the edge of the fire and Henson came forward, stood looking down at them for a moment. 'What's this I hear?' he demanded. 'Putting guards on the train through the night?'

'That's right,' said Bowie without looking up. 'I think it would be the wisest thing to do. We could arrange it so that everyone stood guard for two hours and then woke the next man.'

Henson paused for a moment, then lowered himself heavily to the ground, his face etched with shadow in the flickering firelight. He nodded slowly and it was almost as if he had been expecting this. 'See to it,' he said to Fallon. 'Bowie's right. There's no point in leaving ourselves open to attack.'

'I'll take the first watch,' offered Fallon.

'You know how to handle a gun?' It was a superfluous question, but Bowie knew that it was the only way to bring home the very real danger of their position to these men. A careless man could be a very dead one.

'Wake me at midnight,' Bowie said. 'I'll follow you. And be sure that you keep your eyes and ears open all of the time. These men can creep up on you like rattlers, without any warning.'

Bowie came awake a little before midnight, stirred a little in his blankets and listened to the faint sound as Fallon moved around the perimeter of the camp. The dark silence seemed to be made more intense by that faint whisper of sound; a lonely man with a rifle moving from one wagon to another, eyes peering into the night blackness, hoping to spot any moving shadow before he got a knife in his back. What driving force brought men and women like this out here? he wondered idly, coming across a thousand miles of desert and wilderness, rivers in flood and long stretches of only burning alkali dust. It had to be something stronger than even the desire for life itself; because they must surely have known, even before they set out, that others had tried this before them and now their bones lay bleached in the sun and the dust. He rolled over on his side, heard Fallon pause in the distance, then move on again, satisfied. The fire was down now; only glowing embers that pulsed brighter whenever a stray gust of wind caught at them, but gradually greying to ashes.

There was the soft sound of footsteps approaching. Fallon stood over him, bent to touch his shoulder, then straightened as Bowie rolled out of his blankets and got to his feet, shivering a little as the cold night air caught him.

'Nothing happening,' murmured the other softly. 'Caught a glimpse of something a while back, but I figure it must've been a bear. Never came close enough for me to recognise it.'

The other nodded. 'Could have been a bear,' he said softly. 'I've heard of one or two in these parts. So long as it wasn't some outlaw looking us over.'

He reached for his rifle, hefted it into his right hand, then stepped away from the other and moved as silently as a shadow towards the nearest wagon, stepping over the tongue, out beyond it. The moon floated free of cloud, sailing serenely into the wide heavens. Its light flooded the scene in front of him and gave everything an eerie glow. He threw a quick glance all about him. There was very little cover close at hand; they had chosen this camp site carefully and any man edging forward would have to cross that intervening stretch of open ground before he got close enough to do any real damage.

About two hundred yards away, a thick clump of maple grew atop a low rise, further along the seepage stream where it wound its way downward from that small promontory of ground. It seemed the only place where anyone could lie up and keep a watch on the camp without being seen themselves. He circled the rim of the camp slowly. The darkness that covered the world now, sharpened it seemed by the myriad points of light in the immense vault of the heavens, crowded in on him from the far horizons and he felt something of that deep and enduring loneliness which must have troubled primitive man so many millions of years before. Behind him, one of the fires suddenly burned brighter, casting its red-yellow glow over the wagons next to it. He turned abruptly, saw the man – he did not recognise him from that distance in the darkness – move back to his wagon and climb wearily on to the tongue, looking about him for a moment at the dark, night world, before he lowered his head and moved back inside. The crackle of the flames reached Bowie easily in the clinging stillness.

Minutes ticked away into the dark eternity. The moon drifted behind a bank of cloud, throwing darkness over the land. One of the oxen stirred near the wagons, turned, then bedded itself down again. Pausing on the rim of the wagons, Bowie glanced again in the direction of the clump of maple, standing out like a dark, irregular patch of shadow on the horizon. Was there a movement there, almost as if a horse had suddenly edged from the shelter of the trees, down on to the slope. He narrowed his eyes, swung his gaze a little. At that moment, the moon slipped from behind the bank of cloud and in the flooding light, he saw that he had not been mistaken.

For a second, he paused, then moved quickly between two of the wagons and went over to where Henson's wagon stood near the fire. The other grunted a little as Bowie touched him on the shoulder, then came instantly awake, one hand reaching out for the rifle which lay nearby,

Sitting up, Henson murmured throatily: 'What is it? Time for my watch?'

'Almost,' whispered Bowie. 'I spotted somebody watching us from the maple yonder. I figure I'd better go over and take a look. Keep watch here just in case it is trouble.'

'Want me to come with you? There may be more than you can handle.'

'No. If there are, then you'll still be here to give the warning to the others.'

Before the other could protest, Bowie moved quickly across the clearing, wriggled between two wagons, then slithered out into the rough ground that lay immediately beyond their camp. He could see no sign of the horse now. For a moment he wondered if he had really seen it, or whether he had been mistaken. In the pale yellow moonlight, it was easy to mistake any shadow for an Indian or an outlaw poised to strike. On the other hand, whoever was up there, could have pulled that horse back under cover.

He deliberately circled away from the wagons, moved around to the right of the small grove on top of the rise, keeping his body low, moving without a single sound, like a cat in the stillness. He had left his rifle and pistol behind, had only the broad-bladed knife in his belt, the weapon he always carried with him now, since he had designed that particular shape of blade for his own use.

In spite of this, he felt inwardly confident that he could take whoever was up there completely by surprise. They would be intent on watching the wagons, trying to assess the force which was down there, and he doubted if they had seen him move away into the coarse grass and the bushes that grew alongside the seepage spring.

There was a low gully that angled from where he lay up the side of the slope in the opposite direction to that in which the camp lay. They would not be watching this direction, he told himself grimly. He felt the need for haste now, knowing that if these men did not intend to attack that night, but were only there to spy on the camp, then they might move off at any moment, and on horseback, he would be unable to catch them. Just as he had reasoned, there was no one in sight at the back of the maples. The trees thrust themselves up in dark shadow. Ten feet further on, the gully petered out rapidly, but it had taken him far closer than he had ever dared to hope and using what concealment the mesquite bushes offered, he worked his way forward, edging smoothly and silently over the rough, stony ground, moving upslope. As he neared the top, he went forward more cautiously, listening intently for the faintest warning sound from ahead of him.

It came suddenly, so close to where he lay that his

nerves snapped taut like strings in his body. He froze instantly, face pressed tightly into the dirt, flattening himself under a bush of mesquite, mindless of the bare, thorny branches that tore and scratched at his face and the backs of his hands. The men were less than five feet from where he lay, and it seemed incredible that they had not noticed him as he had approached. Now his straining ears picked out small, seemingly meaningless sounds among the trees. There was the unmistakable breathing of horses and the shuffling movements of the men. He began to inch forward, moving through the rough grass like a snake on his belly, making no sound. At the moment, he was still unable to place the men or to see how many there were. Very carefully, he lifted his head, moved his gaze slowly from side to side. Then he saw them. There were two of them, with their mounts hitched to one of the trees to his right. Their backs were to him and it was obvious they were watching the camp below, oblivious to any danger which might come on them from behind.

He plucked the broad-bladed knife from his belt, held it balanced in his right hand as he poised himself. Then he hesitated. There was something oddly familiar about the man nearest him. Here, the moonlight did not manage to filter through the thickly-leafed branches of the trees, but a second later, almost as if aware of Bowie's eyes on him, the other half turned his head and Bowie saw him in profile. For a moment, he stood absolutely still, then he said in a harsh whisper:

'I thought I might find you somewhere like this, Collie.'

The two men whirled swiftly at his words. Out of the corner of his eye, he saw Collie Thorpe bring up the pistol he held in his right hand, then lower it as he recognised him. He took a step forward, lips drawn back over his teeth in a snarling smile.

'So, Jim, we meet again,' he said softly, hoarsely. 'I thought you'd decided to stay back east in New Orleans with that pirate, Lafitte.'

'I decided to come out west,' Bowie told him. He drew

himself erect, continued to watch the others and in the dim light, he saw the look of understanding that came to Thorpe's face.

'Say, you ain't with that wagon train down yonder, are you?'

'That's right, I am.'

'Now that's what I call real luck. We've had it spotted since yesterday. We heard that a big train had pulled out of New Orleans and somehow, we figured they might decide to head this way to Natchitoches, instead of cutting north and going through Natchez. Seems we were right. after all.' He leaned forward, lips twisted into a thin leering grin. 'You know how much gold they got with 'em, Jim?'

'I know they have some, but it ain't going to be the way you're thinking, Collie. I'm with that train for one reason only, to go with them into Tejas. If you've got any idea of attacking it and expecting me to throw in my lot with you, then you'd better forget it.'

The other hesitated at that, face twisted into a scowl, then the grin came back once again and he scratched his chin thoughtfully. 'Now I call that real unfriendly of you, Jim. You didn't think that way when we were together before, or when we worked with Lafitte. What's come over you now? Not decided to go over on to the side of law and order, have you?' He peered closely at Bowie in the dimness.

'Maybe I have at that,' Bowie said evenly. He kept all trace of emotion out of his voice as he spoke. 'Bringing slaves into this country was one thing, but murderin' women and children for gold is another and I don't intend to be a party to it.'

McGee, standing a few feet away, watching Bowie curiously, said flatly. 'You tryin' to tell us that if we attack that train somewhere along the trail, you'll throw in your lot with them, and fight us?' There was a faint note of incredulity in his hoarse tone.

'That's right,' Bowie nodded, not letting his gaze move

from Thorpe. He knew the other to be the more dangerous and cunning of the two, knew that this man would not hesitate to shoot him in the back if he thought there might be a chance of getting away with it. But Thorpe was also aware of Bowie's reputation on the frontier and he was not willing to risk everything in a foolish attempt to kill the other.

'You've gone soft for some reason,' muttered Thorpe, his eyes glittering in his head. 'I always did reckon it was a mistake to let you stay back there. I figured Lafitte might harden you to the idea of killing, but it seems I was wrong. But I think it only fair to warn you, that we have other men with us, we ain't working this alone. How else do you think we knew the time when this train pulled out of New Orleans?'

'So you've got other men with you,' murmured Bowie tautly. 'I didn't think you'd be so stupid as to try to take the train yourselves. But you won't have many. Everybody will be watching the Natchez Trace. The pickings along this trail will be far too lean for most of 'em.'

He saw from the sudden change of expression on the other's face that his point had been valid and that it had gone home.

'You don't mean to heed this warnin' then?'

Bowie shook his head. 'I'd advise you not to try it,' he said ominously. 'If you do, then you may find you've bitten off more'n you can chew.'

He stepped back slowly, his right hand very close to his belt. He saw Thorpe's glance drop to where the knife rested, could guess what sort of ideas were running through the other's mind at that moment. The other knew that he would be dead with a knife in his chest before he could pluck the pistol clear of his belt, but for a moment, the idea lived in his mind. Then he thrust it away. Forcing the grin back on to his face, he said thinly: 'We'll remember this, Jim. When the time comes, you'll regret it, believe me.'

'Perhaps. But somehow, I don't think so.' Bowie stood

quite still for a moment on the edge of the trees. Then he jerked a thumb in the direction of the waiting horses a few yards away. 'Reckon you'd better mount up and ride out that way.' He nodded towards the rocky slope on the opposite side of the knoll to that where the wagons lay. 'They're watching from down yonder and if they spot you, they may decide to ride after you.'

McGee started towards his horse, then paused as Thorpe said craftily, 'I reckon they'd also know that you were in cahoots with us if we rode the other way. It wouldn't be easy for you to explain to those friends of yours down there how you came to be parleying with a couple of outlaws in the middle of the night, and then let us ride on out without tryin' to stop us. That would look too curious, wouldn't it?'

'Maybe so.' Bowie nodded, feeling the tightness grow in him. 'But it would make very little difference as far as either of you were concerned. You'd both be dead before you could do any talking.'

The other's dark eyes glittered in his face. He seemed on the point of saying something, then thought better of it, closed his teeth with a snap and whirled on his heel, moving back into the tangle of undergrowth towards his horse. Swinging himself up into the saddle, he waited for McGee to do likewise, then leaned forward so that his face was almost level with Bowie's and said throatily: 'I won't forget this, Jim. Believe me, I'll make you pay for it, and soon. You'll begin to wish that you'd killed us here when you had the chance.' There was the promise of death in his voice.

Touching spurs to his mount's flanks, he eased the horse forward, down the slope and out across the flat, rocky ground that lay beyond. Bowie stood still in the shadow of the trees, watching the two riders until they had vanished from sight. Only then did he turn and make his way slowly down to the wagon train.

Someone had thrust more dry wood on to the three fires and they were blazing brightly as he made his way into the clearing. Henson, with his rifle held in the crook of his arm, stepped forward, his face in shadow. It was difficult to read the expression on his broad features.

'Must have been mistaken,' he said softly. 'I reckon it could only have been a bear.'

Henson's shoulders slumped a little but he did not relax fully. He said: 'I still don't like this. I've got a feeling somethin' is goin' to break – and soon.'

Two days later, they moved out of the barren flat country and came to where a wide river ran across their trail. On either side, the banks rose steep and rocky and there was no chance of taking the wagons across at that point. It had rained the previous afternoon and through the night the storm had lashed them, lightning lancing across the berserk heavens, the thunder rolling under the racing black clouds that had come sweeping up from the horizon shortly after noon. A solid blanket of rain had struck the wagons as the dark curtain had drowned out the yellow sunlight. Heads down, the oxen had ploughed their way forward through dust turned suddenly into mud, with runnels of water racing across the track.

Bowie raced his mount along the entire length of the train, urging the drivers to hurry. Thunder rode with him, sometimes cracking like pistol shots in the heavens, and at others, muttering in deep, rumbling rolls which seemed to continue for minutes. There had been little sleep during the long night; not with lightning forking and dancing across the heavens as the storm vent its fury on them. Canvas sagged and whipped as the rain soaked through it, as the wind caught the heavy, cumbersome sheets and threw them in all directions. Under one of the wagons, Bowie had tried to find a dry spot for his bed, but it had been out of the question. The wind and the teeming rain had found every spot, worked its way into his blankets and clothing, until he was wet to the skin. Had there been a protecting ledge of rock or a hill to provide shelter, it might not have been so bad, but here there was only open, flat ground, providing no shelter from the wind and rain, and he had lain there in resignation, listening to the drumming of the rain against the flapping canvas over his head and on the ground. The fires burned only dimly and fitfully that night, hissing as the heavy raindrops fell on to them. Long before morning, they were piles of grey ash and unburnt branches.

Now, at mid-morning, the rain had gone, the storm had cleared the sky and the hot sun brought all of the moisture steaming from the wagons and the ground around them. The rocks danced and shivered in the strong sunlight, the water in the river sparkled brilliantly. Bowie sat tall in the saddle on top of a flat outcrop of rock and stared about him. This was a bad, wild river when in full flood and there had clearly been heavy rain further in the mountains, sending the water rushing and foaming downstream, surging along the high banks, bringing logs down with it. There were rocks out in the middle of the river and the water split around them, racing swiftly and savagely past them, bubbling and frothing. Occasionally, a heavy log, drifting with the current would be smashed against one of the sharp-edged rocks, would rear high into the air before crashing down again.

'We'll never get the wagons across there,' said Henson harshly. He stood on the rock beside Bowie and stared out across the rumbling, rushing waters of the river.

Bowie nodded. 'There'll be a fording place downstream a piece,' he said quietly and with confidence. 'The river's swollen with the recent rains, and we'll have to make a detour here, turn the wagons.'

'How far?'

Bowie shrugged. 'Difficult to say. She's running high. Could be a couple of miles from here, maybe ten. I'll take a ride out.'

Spurring his bay, he moved downstream, keeping as close to the bank as he could but in places, the going was too dangerous, even for a horse, and he was forced to work away from the bank, although the rushing roar of the river in his ears, told him where it lay and he was never very far from it. He rode for five miles before there was any break in the rough ground. Then the rocks fell away and he came to the point where the river, high and swollen, had gouged a wide section from loose ground. He sat for a moment, contemplating the scene. There would be danger here too, of course. As far as a river such as this was concerned, there was always some danger when it was running as high and as fast as this, but it was perhaps the only crossing place for fifty or a hundred miles in either direction. If they were careful, they should make the crossing safely. There were no rocks out there as far as he could see and although the water was deep, the river bed looked smooth and sandy.

He rode back along the way he had come, explained the position to Henson. Slowly, the line of wagons was turned, they moved back a little way from the river to get out of the rocks, then turned south towards the natural ford. They reached it an hour later, stood on the nearer bank while Henson and Fallon strode forward, stood with legs braced well apart, staring out over the river. Finally, Henson nodded his head as though satisfied, came back.

'We'll cross here,' he said tightly. 'Better check all of the wagons before we start.'

The first wagon entered the water. The oxen hit the rush of the current, hesitated for a moment, then thrust forward, urged on by the long bull-whip in Henson's left hand, his right gripping the reins. Ponderously, swaying precariously from side to side as the full weight of that rushing water caught it, the wagon moved into midstream. For a breathless moment, it seemed that it must surely tilt and fall. The oxen struggled to keep their balance, then inch by inch, they dragged it forward, towards the opposite bank, heads low, shoulder muscles bunched under the brown skin.

Slowly, painfully slowly, wheels creaking ominously, canvas dragging in the boiling, turbulent water, the wagon moved up on to the dry land on the far side of the river. No sooner was it there, than the second moved on into the flood and then the third. Drivers standing braced on the tongues of the wagons, hands holding the reins in an iron grip, lashing the oxen as they faltered, sending them on into the river. Bowie sat on the nearer bank until the last wagon had gone into the water, then put his mount forward and rode alongside it. Fallon stood braced with the reins and beside him, holding on to the sides, his wife sat, her face rigid and still, trying not to show the fear which must have been in her mind at that moment. Bowie caught a fragmentary glimpse of the two children in the back, both girls, one ten and the other eight, their faces pale blurs m the dimness. Shaking and swaying, the wagon moved across. Not until everyone was safe on dry land on the far side, did Bowie let his breath go naturally.

He had expected trouble, even there; not only trouble from the river, although that could have been bad enough, but trouble of a far different kind.

Somewhere along this trail, possibly very close at that moment, Collie Thorpe and McGee, and any other outlaws they had joined, would be waiting; and it had come to him that the ideal time and place for them to have attacked the train would have been there, when they had all been intent on the river crossing.

Beyond the river, lay the wide grasslands. Someday, there would be large towns and cities here, railroads and highways. But now there was nothing but the vast, stretching prairie.

Darkness drifted in from the eastern horizon that night and twin threads of smoke rose up from the cook fires in the middle of the ring of wagons. There was a new feeling among the men and women now. Bowie could sense it as he squatted beside Henson, with the rest of the man's family around the fire. The feeling that maybe they had crossed the worst stretch of their journey and that from this moment on things were going to get better, and not worse. They had heard tales of the wild Indians who roamed this part of the territory, of the outlaws who attacked the wagons moving west. So far, they had seen little to indicate they would be troubled by either and their spirits were rising with every mile they travelled. Only Bowie, seated just inside the ring of light from the fire, felt troubled and worried in his mind. Where were Collie Thorpe and McGee at that moment? he wondered. Had they watched while they had moved south, off the trail, and forded the river? Were they behind them, or somewhere ahead along the trail – or was it possible that, at that very moment, they were moving up on them out of the darkness?

Apprehensively, he glanced beyond the fireglow, beyond the ring of wagons, towards the timber that stretched close to the trail at this point. He would have preferred to have continued on for another mile or so into more open country where it would have been more difficult for any attacker to take them by surprise, but the oxen were tired after that river crossing, the men too.

That night, Bowie slept dry near one of the wagons. There was little movement in the camp. Two men were keeping guard now. Henson had looked curiously at Bowie when he had insisted that the guard be doubled during the night, but he had made no protest. Had he been thinking of that night when Bowie had gone out into the brush and stayed out there for close on half an hour, after he had thought he had spotted movement there? If he had been turning that over in his mind, his grim face had not betrayed anything of it.

What woke Bowie during the night, he wasn't sure. Maybe it had been the stone grinding in the small of his back under the blanket. He lay for a moment, staring up at the sky over his head, the moon riding high and full, every sense stretched to its limit as he strove to pick out anything out of the ordinary. For a long moment, he could hear nothing. Nearby, one of the fires had burned low and the other was fading at the far side of the ring.

Slowly and silently, he pushed himself up on one elbow, peering about him into the moon-thrown shadows. Nothing moved as far as he could see. Letting his gaze swing around the wagons, standing out clearly in the flooding moonlight, he tried to make out the shapes of the two men who were supposed to be on watch. When he failed to see them, it came to him that there was something wrong. Like a ghost, he rose to his feet, one hand touching first the loaded pistol and then the knife in his belt. Wraith-like, he went to the nearest wagon, ducked under it, paused for a moment and stared about him. A dark shadow lay humped on the ground a few yards to his left. Wriggling forward, he came up to it, turned the man over.

There was the wet stickiness of blood on the other's back and although the body was still warm, there was no heartbeat in the wrist, no pulse that Bowie could detect.

He did not doubt that the same thing had happened to the other guard, possibly on the far side of the ring of wagons. They had not heard their attackers gliding up on them from behind, had been easy targets for men with knives.

Getting to his feet, he moved into the shadow thrown by the wagon, pressing his body tightly against the canvas. It was odd that the outlaws – for such he felt sure they were, since an Indian, especially a Choctaw, would have scalped the dead guard – had not attacked now that they had killed the guards. Maybe they had sent in one man to deal with any guards and were now crouched out there in the timber, ready to attack in force.

The trees stood in dark shadow less than fifty yards away. A swift glance told Bowie that this was the most possible place where they were hiding. It was certainly the only place which would have hidden a large group of men. Even as he watched, the moonlight picked out a dark shape that glided from a mound less than twenty yards away. He caught a glimpse of the man's head and shoulders as the other slithered forward through the tall grass. Without pausing to think, Bowie pulled the pistol from his belt, checked it, then took careful aim and pulled the trigger. The dark shadow threw up its arms and yelled loud and long as it fell forward out of sight. Even before the echoes of the single shot had died away, Bowie was reloading the pistol and the camp came awake. Then, from the trees where he had guessed the outlaws were hiding, came the savage yells as men ran out into the open, men who knew that their plan to take the wagon train completely by surprise had failed, who knew that their only chance of success now lay in killing the defenders before they could collect their scattered wits and rub the sleep from their eyes.

Crouching down, Bowie sent a second shot into the group of men who came running and leaping over the uneven ground. It was difficult to aim properly in the moonlight. There were far too many shadows at which to fire and it was essential that every shot should find its mark. He saw one of the men throw up his hands to his face, sway drunkenly, the pistol dropping from nerveless fingers as he reeled back with blood streaming down his face.

By now, several of the other men were wide awake, had taken their rifles and were firing at the running yelling men. A long rifle was thrust suddenly from the canvas flap of the nearest wagon. Bowie had a brief glimpse of the girl who crouched there, holding the rifle in both hands, her face filled with a look of fear. But she aimed the weapon slowly and pulled the trigger. The recoil almost knocked her off her feet, but one of the running men was hit in mid-leap as he tried to negotiate an outcrop of rock. He seemed to twist like a cat in mid-air, then flopped limply on to the edge of the rock. His head struck it with a sickening, hollow sound and his body rolled a couple of feet before it came to rest. Bowie ignored him. There had been nothing wrong with the woman's aim. Already, the attacking outlaws were fanning out, realising that there was little sense in making a frontal attack which was sure to be expensive. They went under cover now and began crawling forward, firing as they came. There was the vicious shriek of metal hitting one of the uprights of the wagon behind which Bowie crouched and he pulled himself instinctively down, ducking his head as the metal flicked close to his skull and hummed into the distance.

Henson was yelling orders on the far side of the camp. Out of the corner of his eye, Bowie saw him moving the men into position. Clearly he recognised the danger and was making certain that the entire ring of wagons was guarded, giving the outlaws no chance to move in and take them from the centre.

The firing from the wagons was slow and deliberate and steady now. Every one was awake and had recognised their danger. Crouching down, Bowie glanced between the wooden wheels, trying to make out where the main enemy thrust was likely to come. He had an advantage that the others in the train did not have. He knew Collie Thorpe and McGee, knew how they worked, how they thought and planned. He guessed that they would work their men around the wagon train to make sure they drew as much defensive fire as possible, forcing them to thin out their men, but they would be holding a handful in reserve, ready to throw them at what they considered to be the weakest point in the defensive circle. Once they broke through, it would mean the end for the men and women defending the wagons, and it was essential that he, Bowie, should know where the attackers meant to launch that assault and be ready to meet it. He guessed that it would come from the opposite side to that from which the first attack had come, so as to confuse them.

Out of the moonlit darkness, a hoarse voice yelled: 'Somebody get a fire goin' and put a torch to that canvas.' It sounded like Thorpe's voice, but he could not be certain, nor could he be sure just where the other was.

Crawling forward, he waited until he made out the man who crouched less than ten yards away with flint and steel. Before the other could start a fire in the dry grass, a shot rang out from one of the wagons and the man keeled over as if he had been struck on the side of the head with a mighty fist. He lay still in the moonlight and Bowie was dimly aware of Thorpe cursing somewhere off to the right.

A man came running over from behind Bowie, crouched down beside him, breathing hard. 'See anythin' out there?' he asked in a harsh tone. 'I thought I heard somebody yellin'.'

Bowie nodded. 'That you, Fallon?' he said softly.

'That's right.' The other moved closer to him, the pistol in the right hand glinting in the moonlight.

'How's everythin' on the other side?'

'We've got 'em pinned down yonder. Couldn't tell how many there are, but I reckon that shot which woke us up, must've saved it. If they had caught us asleep then we would have been—' He broke off sharply. 'What happened to Keller and Dunston? They was supposed to be on guard.'

'Dunston's over yonder with a knife-wound in his back. I reckon the same thing happened to Keller though I ain't seen him.'

'God.' The other muttered the single word through his clenched teeth. 'Knifed in the back and when they was supposed to be keeping a look out for somethin' like this.'

'These men can move like ghosts when they have a need to,' Bowie said softly. He glanced up, squinting against the moonlight, then caught the other's arm in a tight grip. 'Here comes the big attack. Better make sure that you shoot straight. Don't bother to reload your pistol. Use your knife. It's quicker.'

He wasn't sure whether Fallon was the kind of man who could use a knife in this way, but right now there was no time to worry on that particular score. The men were moving in now, creeping from one concealing shadow to another, taking care not to expose themselves to the steady and generally accurate fire from the wagons facing them.

Bowie waited until they were less than ten yards away, then sighted his pistol on the leading man, squeezed the trigger gently. The weapon bucked slightly his hand and the man collapsed in an ungainly heap, going down without a murmur. The others came rushing forward, firing as they ran. Here, the ground was uneven and the moonlight made it difficult to pick out any obstacles there.

Without pausing to reload the pistol, Bowie pulled the knife from his belt and rose lithely to his feet. Beside him, Fallon aimed and fired, the flash of the pistol a brilliant lance of flame in the dimness.

One of the men fell sideways with a grunt of pain as Bowie launched himself forward, striking hard and accurate with the knife. He felt it strike flesh and bone. The man tried to bring up his pistol, but his eyes were glazing swiftly and the life went out of him with a long sigh as he fell forward, slumping against Bowie's knees. Two other men rushed past him in the moonlight. Dimly, he was aware of Fallon shouting harshly, but before he could turn to help the other, a dark shape came lunging forward. In the moonlight, he recognised Thorpe a second before the other saw him. The moon was in Bowie's eyes and he moved around the other, circling him. He saw Thorpe's hand come up, holding the pistol and instinctively, he twisted to one side. The shot sounded oddly loud in his ears and something scorched painfully along his left arm, cutting across the fleshy part. Thorpe knew in that second that he had missed and his hand swung down for his own knife, a long, slender bladed weapon thrust down into his belt at his hip, like a sword. It glinted bluely in the moonlight as he came for Bowie, lips twisted back to reveal his uneven teeth.

'I warned you what would happen, Jim, if we ever met again,' he hissed tightly. 'I'm goin' to kill you now.' He swung with the knife, flashing it in front of Bowie's face, deliberately missing with that swing. But Bowie knew better than to let his glance follow the shining arc of the knife. He kept his glance on the other's face, his eyes deliberately unfocused, so that he was ready and waiting when Thorpe stepped forward, ready to deal the death blow, seeking to find a spot where life lay close to the surface.

A quick thrust and Bowie's knife drew a thin line of

blood from the other's forearm. Almost, the other dropped the knife as he took a step backward in sudden surprise and pain. Then he grinned viciously. 'You still know some of your old tricks,' he rasped, 'but they won't save you now.'

Swaying his head to one side, the other swung with his left hand, and for the first time, Bowie saw that he had carried two knives. Now he held one in each hand and there was an expression of triumph on his face as he moved forward. But he had been careless and a quick movement to one side forced him to turn with his face towards the moon. Bowie saw him blink his eyes suddenly as he strove to focus them in the strong light. The other was at a momentary disadvantage and Bowie took full use of it. Moving in under the other's upraised arm, he swung sharply and with all of his weight behind the blow. The knife took Thorpe in the chest, went in up to the hilt. For a long moment, he stood perfectly still, eyes wide and staring, fixed on Bowie's face with a look of utter astonishment in them as if unable to believe what had happened. Then he uttered a long sigh, deep in his throat, pitched forward on to his knees, arms outstretched as if to grasp his adversary by the legs. One knife, still clutched in his fingers, buried itself in the soft ground as he fell. The other spun from his fingers and flew in a glittering arc into a nearby bush.

Bowie drew himself up to his full height, stared about him for any sign of further danger, saw that there was no one else left standing and moved back to the nearest wagon. The firing had almost ceased now, with only an occasional desultory shot ringing out, mainly from the far side of the ring of wagons. He guessed that some of the men, still trigger happy after the attack, were merely firing at shadows, taking no chances.

Going forward, he found Fallon leaning against the wheel of the wagon as if tired. Then he noticed the blood on the other's shirt, placed his hand under the man's arm and helped him inside the protective ring of wagons. Only then was he aware of the sudden silence and the fact that his arm was stiff and sticky with blood.

No one slept that night, but there were no further attacks on the train. The few outlaws who had escaped, were evidently headed away from that place, not wishing to take any further chances with the wagon train. Both Collie Thorpe and McGee had been killed during the fighting and early the next morning, before they moved out, their own dead were buried, the two guards and three others, a man and two of the women, and Henson said the words over the shallow graves, reading from a much tattered and dog-eared black Bible. In the hot sunlight, it seemed an oddly unreal scene to Bowie, listening to that suddenly quiet, serious voice, speaking of the death which lay around them even in life, and of the hope of another life yet to come.

Closing the Bible with a snap, Henson turned and moved away, cast a quick glance over the waiting wagons with the oxen and horses already hitched into the traces. 'All right,' he said in a loud tone. 'Let's move out of this place.'

'What about those other dead?' asked Bowie softly. 'What do we do with them?'

'We leave them where they are,' declared the other emphatically. 'They chose their way of life and their way of death. They will find no mercy with the Lord.'

Bowie swung up into the saddle, stared at the other's unbending features for a long moment, then gave a brief, slight nod. Wheeling his mount, he rode on ahead of the wagon train, moving forward into the stretching vastness of the country that lay before them, shimmering a little in the heat, but still fresh in the early morning sunlight.

The days drew into a steady routine. As they drove westward, the land changed its character. They came to a stretching desert filled with buttes and mesas which had become fluted and shaped by long ages of wind and rain, or abrading dust which had worn away even the sandstone. There was mesquite here and patches of low cactus and scrub oak, and little water. Many of the water holes they did find were nothing more than dried-up hollows in the ground, where the soil around them had become cracked and baked by the tremendous heat of the sun. It was a wild and inhospitable country, one they crossed as quickly as they could. On the far rim of the desert, they ran into low foothills and then taller mountains, moving through narrow gorges and passes which in turn led them out towards the flatter country around Natchitoches.

Then, on the fifteenth day after they had set out from New Orleans, they drove into Natchitoches itself. There were French soldiers and Spaniards here, but already they were moving out, as the Americans came in. A restless, uneasy town on the very edge of the Twilight Strip that lay to the west toward Tejas.

4
FRONTIERSMAN

Most of the French had moved out of Louisiana, but there were still some officials left in Natchitoches. Pierre Leroux was a slightly-built figure, still resplendent in his uniform, who greeted Bowie and Henson courteously, motioned them to a chair.

'I must apologise for the confusion here, but now that Louisiana is a part of the United States, the French will be moving out. There are very few of us left now, but we still have our uses here and those of us who wish to remain have been granted permission to do so.' He placed the tips of his fingers together, regarded them closely over his hands. 'You say that you wish to go on to Nacogdoches. But that is across the frontier in Mexican territory. In Tejas.'

'We know that,' said Henson, nodding slowly. 'But we heard back East that the authorities there are willing to allow folk to move in, that they grant them land to work, as farmers.'

Leroux raised his brows slightly, regarded the other closely, then pursed his lips tightly together, seemed to mull the thought over in his mind for a while, before answering. 'I've heard that too, but conditions in Tejas change abruptly and without warning these days. We here in Natchitoches only know what we hear from men who've been there and then came back. Unfortunately, there are very few, unless they are outlaws, and we do not want these men back here.'

'But you must have heard something,' put in Bowie.

The other switched his gaze to him. 'We hear a little, disconnected stories which can be put together to give us some kind of picture as to conditions there. We know that Spanish influence has been declining rapidly in Tejas and in Mexico. There was a revolt there led by Miguel Hidalgo y Costilla over seventeen years ago.'

'But other things have happened since then, particularly along the eastern border with Louisiana.'

'That is true. Since Louisiana was purchased by the United States, there have been several expeditions crossing into Tejas over the Twilight Strip. This – how do you call it – no man's land, is a springboard for these men who would apparently be wishing to establish an independent republic there. Certainly, in the past they have fought against Spain, helping the Mexicans, but I am not blinded by this myself. I believe that they really wish to bring Tejas under the United States.'

Bowie nodded. It made sense from what he had been able to learn along the frontier. There had been talk of a colony being established on the Brabos seven years before and since then there had been this rapid colonisation.

'I understand that the Mexican authorities have been giving land grants to both their own nationals and to Americans, but there have been difficulties recently.'

'Difficulties?' asked Henson.

'*Oui*. There has been talk that the American population of Tejas has been growing so rapidly during the past six or seven years, that the Mexican Government is becoming distrustful and will not grant many more of these land grants to men much as yourselves. I think they fear that America will take over Tejas on the pretext that the population is now more American than Mexican.'

'Can you be sure of this?' demanded Henson tightly. From the expression on his face, Bowie guessed that the other could see his chance of getting land in Tejas slipping away from his grasp.

Leroux spread his hands in a gesture of resignation. 'Who can be sure of anything in a case like this, *Monsieur*?'

Henson sank back in his chair. 'I understand. But we will be given permission to go on to Nacogdoches?'

'I can give you a pass to take yourselves and all those on your wagons through to Nacogdoches,' nodded the other. 'But with things as they are, I cannot tell you how far you will get with such a pass.'

'We'll get far enough,' said the other harshly. 'We've come all the way from east of New Orleans and we don't intend to let anythin' stop us now.'

Leroux smiled faintly. 'I hope that you are right, *Monsieur*. But this is a dangerous strip of territory. There are more outlaws and cut-throats to the kilometre there than anywhere else in this country. There are not many wagon trains get through without trouble.'

'We've met trouble and we can take care of ourselves,' declared Henson.

Leroux glanced at Bowie. 'Do you intend to go on with these people, Monsieur Bowie?' he asked. 'Forgive me for saying it, but you do not look like a farmer.'

'I'm not. But I figure they may have a place for a man like myself out in Tejas. It's a new country and I've always had a hankering for something like that.'

Leroux's brows went up a little further. 'I see.' He shrugged. 'Provided you intend to keep the law when you get there, I see no difficulty.'

He pulled a pad towards him. 'If you will give me the names of everyone travelling with you, I'll make out the necessary documents. These should be given to the Commandant at Nacogdoches. Whether he will be Spanish or Mexican, I do not know. That is something you will have to discover for yourselves when you arrive there.'

Henson took the pass, folded it carefully and pushed it deeply into his pocket. The commandant turned to Bowie. 'I have not included your name on that pass, *Monsieur*. I will issue you with a separate one as you will probably not be continuing with these people once you reach Nacogdoches.' He scribbled his name at the bottom of the document, handed it to Bowie.

Outside, in the dusty street, the two men paused, looking about them. Then Henson said: 'There is one thing which has been puzzling me for several days, Mister Bowie. I wonder if you would care to tell me, now that we have reached Natchitoches in safety.'

Bowie glanced at the other closely, trying to read the expression on the other's face, but it was as inscrutable as ever. 'What is it?' he asked.

'Those outlaws who attacked us the night after we forded the river. I've had the feeling, without any proof of course, that some of them were known to you.' His lips were pressed tightly together, eyes slitted a little.

Bowie hesitated, not sure whether or not to tell the other the truth, or try to lie. Then he nodded his head slowly. 'I had met up with two of those men before. I knew they would be watching one of the trails west, but I felt sure they would be to the north, around Natchez. That's why I persuaded you to go the other way. I suppose you can say that those who died in your wagon train, died because of me.'

'I'm not blaming you for that,' said the other gruffly. If he felt any surprise at what Bowie had admitted, he gave no outward sign of it. 'You gave as good as you got when they did attack.' He let his gaze drift back to Bowie's face. 'They were there some nights earlier, before they attacked, were they not?'

'You seem to know a lot,' said Bowie thinly. 'Yes, that night I rode out of the camp to check on the movement I saw among the trees. I bumped into them there. They were watching the camp, trying to discover how many men you had riding with you. I warned them that if they did decide to attack you, I'd fight them.'

'I see. I thought that might be it.' Henson drew deeply on his cigar, stood for a long moment, staring down at it.

Then he tossed the glowing end to the ground and stepped on it with his moccasin.

'We'll need to get supplies here. There won't be any place to get more between here and Nacogdoches. I reckon we'll be ready to move out in three days' time.'

Two days after leaving Natchitoches, Bowie rode across a wide ridge, five miles ahead of the slower-moving wagon train. Burdened with supplies, the wagons creaked along the narrow trail. Here, they were on a trail that had been used by many wagon trains as they passed westward, a trail easily picked out.

Riding down the far side of the ridge, he came to a spread of timber. At first they were only willows, small saplings, but these grew taller by steps until he was soon in thick timber. Most of it was old, first-growth pine here, massive and strong at the butt and rising in a smooth line towards the thick top covering which completely shut out the sun, with only a faint green light managing to filter through into the brush. There was the sharply refreshing smell of old needles on the ground, making a thick carpet on which his horse made no sound as it moved forward.

He knew little of this land, yet inwardly, he felt no concern. He had lived in country such as this all of his life, felt at home in the pattern of hills and forests, deserts and wide, rushing rivers. There was plenty of wild game here. He saw their sign everywhere he went, knew they would not be short of food all the way into Nacogdoches.

By the time he got back, the others had halted, wagons drawn in a single file, while the women cooked the midday meal. Bowie ate his slowly. This was the dangerous Twilight Country, between Louisiana and Tejas; country which belonged to no one but the lawless, the ideal breeding ground for the worst outlaws known in the whole of the bloody history of this land.

Fallon sank down beside him, spooning the food into his hungry mouth. Not until the plate was clean did he speak. 'You reckon we'll get through to Nacogdoches, Bowie?'

'I think so. This is bad country, full of outlaws. We may run into trouble as we did before, since this is the only trail that every wagon train takes goin' through into the Tejas country.'

'You see anythin' when you were scoutin'?'

'Nothin'. Tracks of some bear and deer. We won't go short on food.'

The other did not look entirely satisfied. 'The commandant at Natchitoches warned us that we would run into trouble along this trail. Reckoned that some of the outlaws operatin' in these parts were known to go into Natchitoches and get information on trains pullin' out westward.'

'That makes sense,' Bowie agreed. He knew that the other was now seeking some kind of assurance. But it was somewhat difficult to give such assurance, knowing as he did the multitude of dangers which faced them before they arrived in Nacogdoches. This Sabine wilderness was the haunt of more killers and outlaws than any other part of the vast country which was soon to become the United States. Here, every man made his own law and lived by it. The stream of emigrants into Tejas was growing larger every year, and soon it would become more than a trickle, it would be a mighty flood, sweeping away the Mexican authorities, annexing Tejas into America.

'I'm scared,' admitted the other in a low voice. He turned his head to make sure that Henson had not heard what he said. 'Not scared so much for myself, but for the women and children travelling with us. We know what we're up against and it's a man's part to do this, to push the frontier westward. Sometimes, though, I lie awake at night, unable to sleep, thinking that we will fail them, that we'll all be destroyed long before we reach this promised land everyone seems to be talking of.'

'We'll make it,' Bowie said, forcing conviction into his voice. 'We've got to make it, because if we fail, then all the others who might have followed us, will stay behind, back east, and this country will never expand as it must if it's to become great.'

'But even if we do get through, there was talk in Natchitoches that the Mexican Government may refuse grants to Americans. They say that there are too many Americans there now, that if any more are allowed in, there will be so many that they may attempt to fight the Mexican authorities and take over Tejas for themselves.'

Bowie forced a quick grin. 'There are always rumours like this on the trail,' he pointed out. 'No one knows how they begin, but they become so distorted that it's often impossible to recognise them. There may be a tiny grain of truth in this one, but nothin' more.'

They pushed on for a further fifteen miles that afternoon, driving the oxen to their utmost limit until the beasts bawled in protest as they lurched against the leather traces. The ground roughened considerably and Bowie knew that they were approaching the Calcasieu River, east of the Sabine. That night, he rode the rim of the wagon camp, rode in a wide circle through the quiet darkness. There were fireflies darting through the warm air and over his head, the heavens was a vast powdering of stars, soft and luminous in the spring air. The days and nights were becoming warmer now and although this was a wild country, they still managed to find large stretches of lush green grass for the cattle and horses.

The Neutral Zone itself stretched roughly from the Calcasieu River, over the Sabine and on to the Neches River, almost a hundred miles to the west. Here were gathered the worst elements of human society that any age had brought into being, the lowest possible dregs of mankind. Vicious, hardened men who cared nothing for human life, who killed and plundered often for the very joy of it.

Pulling the lashings of his jacket more tightly, he eased himself into a more comfortable position in the saddle. Breathing in the cool air, he felt it go down into his lungs like wine. This, as far as he was concerned, was the best part of the day. Were it not for the fact that the outlaws always preferred to attack shortly after dark, it would have been perfect. As it was, he found it doubly difficult to relax. It was possible for him to relax his body, tired muscles saw to that; but how to relax the mind, when he knew that the heavy responsibility, that of the lives of every man, woman and child in this entire wagon train lay in his hands.

Riding back to the wagons, he dismounted, slipping wearily from the saddle, led his mount through a narrow gap between two of the wagons, turned it loose in the centre and walked slowly to one of the fires, feeling the warmth of it reach out and envelop him. There was a small group of men seated around the blaze. One of them glanced up as he approached, motioned him down and handed him a mug, pouring some coffee into it from the can over the flames.

'Quiet out there,' said Henson. 'Too damned quiet for my liking.'

Bowie shook his head. 'I figure they'll wait until we reach the Sabine.'

'And if they don't choose to wait?' There was more than just a question in the other's harsh tone.

Bowie lifted his head and stared at him across the fire. 'Then we have to fight them here,' he retorted. 'We have no other choice.'

Morning brought rain; low grey clouds scudding in from the south-west and breakfast was a meal eaten quickly and in discomfort. Men cursed as they struggled to get the bawling oxen into the traces, or hitched the horses to the wagons. Bowie threw an apprehensive glance at the heavens, trying to estimate how long this rain might last. There had been no trace of the sun at dawn. The rolling grey clouds had blotted it out long before sunrise and the entire heavens were an overall grey which portended no early break in the weather. If this happened, it could mean that the Calcasieu River would be full; a wicked river to cross even at the best of times. Now, swollen by the rains, it could be the very devil.

When they reached it, the water was already quite high, rushing swiftly along the banks. Bowie rode back after checking it, his face serious. Henson stood up on the tongue of the lead wagon, drawing himself up to his full height.

'Well?' he demanded.

'We'll have to put them across now,' answered the other. 'If we wait until the rains stop, there could be a delay of several days before the waters subside. With luck, we may make it now – if we hurry.'

The wagons went over half an hour later, with logs lashed to them to float and stabilise them. The crossing was accomplished with less trouble than Bowie had anticipated and they rested for only an hour on the far bank before moving on again; on into the greyness of rain which now blanketed the entire countryside, blinding sheets that lashed at them as the wind strengthened. At times, it was impossible to see more than a hundred yards ahead of them and to ease the strain on the oxen in the treacherous, slippery ground, the men walked in silence beside the wagons, heads down, the water running in rivulets off the wide brims of their hats, soaking into their clothing, working its way into their boots. But there was no time to notice the discomfort. Time only to keep trudging forward, caring little for what went on around them.

That night, there was little talk around the fires. Men ate their evening meal in silence and turned in quickly. The next day would soon come and then another, and there were men who did not really believe that a place such as Nacogdoches, or Tejas existed. It was a myth which lay over the horizon, but which could never be reached.

Wrapped tightly in his blanket, Bowie listened to the steady beat of the rain as it drummed on the ground and the wagon above him. With the wind behind it, there was no place to shelter from the probing rain. He could dimly hear the low voices of the men on guard. Occasionally one of them would move out of the shadows at the edge of the camp, take some of the dry wood from the box strapped under one of the wagons and toss it on to the fire. The flames would blaze up momentarily as they fed on the dry branches. But swiftly, the firelight would dim as the rain came down on it and the orange glow would shrink until there was only a tiny circle around each fire.

There was more rain the next day, but during the afternoon, the sky cleared, the sun came out strongly and they drove on through a barren stretch of country that steamed in the heat as all of the moisture was sucked out of the ground by the fierce sun in half the time that it had taken to fall.

Ten days after they had pulled out of Natchitoches, the wagon train rolled into the streets of Nacogdoches. They were now in Tejas, in Mexican territory. Everywhere there were unmistakable signs of Spanish influence, from the churches to the wide streets and the uniforms of the soldiers. There was no curiosity in the glances of the people on the streets as the wagon train rolled in. Perhaps, thought Bowie, they had seen too many trains such as this arrive, knew what it meant.

Two of the soldiers came forward, stood in the middle of the dusty street, their rifles held ready. One moved up to the wagon, stood beside the tongue, staring up at Henson.

'You are *Americanos*?' he said slowly.

Henson nodded, 'That's right. We have permission to travel here from the commandant at Natchitoches.' He dug into his pocket and pulled out the document, handing it down to the other. The soldier took it, perused it carefully, then nodded and gave it back. 'That would seem to be in order,' he said slowly. He looked at Bowie. 'And you, *Senor*.'

Bowie took out the pass and gave it to the other. The man scrutinised it, then handed it up to him.

'Everything would seem to be in order,' he repeated, 'but you will have to speak with the commandant here. You are travelling further into Tejas?'

Henson nodded. 'We hope to receive land here. We

Bowie of the Alamo

heard that the Mexican Government will sell land to settlers.'

'That may be so. It will depend on the commandant. He will decide who is to be given land and who will not be welcome here.'

The Mexican commandant was dark-featured, slightly-built, with piercing black eyes that missed nothing. He had a small black moustache clearly designed to give him a military appearance and he sat stiffly erect in his chair, face expressionless. The documents which Henson and Bowie had brought with them were on the table in front of him, one slender, well-manicured hand resting on them. He sat quite still for a long moment, his eyes never leaving their faces, then he stirred in his chair and said thinly: 'You realise, of course, that under certain circumstances, the Mexican Government have found it necessary to impose some – ah, restriction, on the immigration of settlers into Tejas. This has been brought about mainly because of the action of your own countrymen I regret that there are those among them, whom we allowed into our country in good faith, who have attempted to incite rebellion against the lawful Government of Tejas.' He smiled thinly, but there was no warmth, no mirth, in it. 'Since France sold the state of Louisiana to the American Government, there have been those elements among the American settlers here who have advocated that Tejas should also become part of the United States. This is, of course, something which my Government cannot tolerate and we have to be extremely careful now whom we allow to enter and settle here. You realise my position, I trust. There are good men and bad men in every country, but we cannot allow the number of *Americanos* to grow more rapidly than that of our own people, otherwise there would be more trouble here than we could handle.'

'We realise that,' said Henson. He frowned and stared directly at the other across the highly polished table. 'All we want is permission to buy land and settle here. It matters nothing to us whether this is Mexican territory or American territory. We're farmers, looking for a place where we can settle, grow our crops and become an accepted part of the community.'

'Very well.' The other appeared to have made a sudden decision. 'I have had your wagons examined – a very necessary formality, I'm afraid, and I am convinced that you are speaking the truth. There are, as you well know, many outlaws operating in the Twilight Strip to the east of Nacogdoches. Only a month ago, three of them were caught and tried here, and sentenced to death. One managed to escape, but the other two were executed. Very often, they attempt to enter Tejas, claiming to be settlers.'

'Then we can have our land?' inquired Henson tautly. There was a look of expectancy on his face.

'Very well, Senor Henson.' The other reached into his drawer, pulled out a seal and methodically heated wax in a small burner, pouring a pool on to the bottom of the paper before impressing the seal on to it. He handed the document back to the other. 'This will take you to Bejar where you will be allocated land according to the number of families in your wagon train.' The other paused, then glanced at Bowie. 'As for you, Senor Bowie, I understand that you do not wish to receive a land grant, that you wish to remain here indefinitely. May I ask what it is you wish to do in Tejas?'

Bowie shrugged. 'This is a new country,' he said easily. 'I'm sure there must be a place for a man who can turn his hand to most anythin'.'

This time, there was a definite smile on the other's face. He sat back in his chair and placed the tips of his fingers together, nodding his head very slowly. 'You are right, of course, Senor. You had better see Henri LaVache. He's concerned with opening up the frontiers in Tejas. As you probably realise, there are vast areas which have not yet been fully explored; not only in the Twilight Strip, but further to the north of Nacogdoches.'

'Henri LaVache,' murmured Bowie. 'He sounds like a Frenchman, not a Mexican.'

'Here you will find men of every conceivable nationality in the service of Mexico. Adventurers, pioneers, men such as yourself.'

For a moment, the Mexican's eyes were shining as hard as the polished mahogany of the desk in front of him. 'If you co-operate with us, I'm sure you will find that we can be very generous,' said the other. 'But I feel it my duty to warn you that there may be trouble here, bad trouble. Almost daily, fighting flares up between *Americanos* and our soldiers. My advice is to keep within the law, to take no sides, and do nothing which could provoke trouble.'

Night reached in from the east and they made camp on the bank of a narrow stream that came tumbling down in a rush of foam from the tall hills that rose to the north. The darkly-wooded slopes had stood in shadow while the crests of the hills were still touched by the last red rays of the setting sun. A deep and intense silence hung over everything, shrouding the four men at the camp as if in a thick blanket. The horses stood tethered a little way off, close by the stream, while the men sat around the fire which had been built in a small clearing.

LaVache rubbed at the beard on his cheeks. His long hair was cut square at the forehead and again at the nape of his neck and his eyes peered out from beneath shaggy brows, drawn together into a straight line as he frowned into the fire.

Across from him sat Aldred and Cain, both men in their late thirties, dark-haired and broadly-built. Watching them unobtrusively, Bowie knew inwardly that only men such as these could exist on this wild and untamed frontier of Tejas. Self-sufficient men who could wrest a living from any kind of land, even one as inhospitable as this. Some day, men would come into this country, open it up from both east and west. There would be trails criss-crossing the tremendous territory. But now, it was virgin land, exactly as it had been for thousands of years, untouched by the hand of man. But if there was to be any advance here, in Tejas, if men and women were to come and batter this country into any sort of shape, men had to go in first, to explore and pioneer, to open up the frontiers.

'There'll be rain before the morning,' Bowie said quietly. He threw a quick glance at the sky overhead. The first stars were showing brightly now, but to the west, there was a low bank of thin cloud that was spreading slowly towards the moon in the south-west.

LaVache nodded, prodded at the fire with a pointed stick, sending a shower of red sparks high into the air where they worked out several feet over their heads.

'I figure there should be a stretch of open ground beyond these hills,' he murmured. 'Never been in these parts before. Do you know this country?' He looked at Bowie, who shook his head.

Cain put coffee in the tin can hanging over the fire, then dragged the deer they had shot earlier that day from the rocks and began to cut up the hams. With his knife, he cut open the tendon under the leg, thrust a heavy branch through and hung the ham over the fire beside the coffee.

'Tomorrow mornin', I suggest we split into two groups and meet on the far side of the hills,' said LaVache. 'There's a lot of ground to cover and we waste time going in one group.'

'You think they'll make a trail through this country?' asked Aldred quietly.

'Could be. If they want to push across Tejas to the west, this is the way they'll come. From what I found out in Nacogdoches, the Mexicans want to build a fort here, keep back the Indians. Unless they do that, they'll never open up the territory.'

'Beats me why they should want to open it up,' grunted Cain thickly. 'You won't get anythin' to grow here.'

There was little further conversation while they ate. Bowie teased through the meat with his knife before slicing it and pushing it into his mouth. It was hot and tough, but he chewed it slowly before swallowing it, washing it down with the hot coffee.

'Funny-lookin' knife you've got there,' remarked LaVache, watching him. 'Don't recollect seein' one like that before – anywhere.'

Bowie handed it over to him and the Frenchman turned it over in his hands, examining it curiously. 'I can see where it would be far more useful than this.' He slid his own knife from his belt, held it out alongside the other.

Giving the broad-bladed knife back to Bowie, he slid his own back into his belt, rubbed the back of his hand across his mouth. There was curiosity in his eyes as he said softly: 'They tell me that you rode in with a bunch of settlers. Any reason why you left them, why you didn't go on south to get some land for yourself?'

Bowie hesitated, then grinned. 'Could be that I prefer to ride the trail, rather than tie myself down to one spot. This is a big country and a man would have to spend two lifetimes to see it all, or as much as he wanted.'

LaVache nodded. 'Perhaps it's better this way. They say there's been more trouble to the south, around Conception. More *Americanos* moving in and trying to claim Tejas for America.' His smile thinned a little as he went on more seriously. 'Mexico will never sell Tejas to America as we sold Louisiana. After all, France is many thousands of miles away and we have little interest here. But they are very close to Tejas and if they have to, they can send their men in and back up their arguments by force.' His eyes were speculative as he went on. 'But already, people are beginning to take sides. That is inevitable. If there is fighting, I wonder which side you will be on, or the rest of us for that matter.'

'When I came to Tejas, the commandant gave me a piece of advice. He said that it would be easier for me if I didn't take sides in any dispute. I think he was right and so far, even though I've been here for three years, I've seen nothing to make me change my mind.'

The other's brows went up a little. 'But it may be that you will think differently once we get back to Nacogdoches. There is a strong movement afoot to drive the Mexicans out of Tejas, to make it a state of America. You are still an American and if fighting does break out, will you stand by and see your countrymen, and their families, wiped out by the Mexicans?'

Bowie stared into the flickering flames of the fire, aware of the heat on his face. There was undoubtedly something in what the other said. Could he stand by and see men and women slaughtered? Americans such as himself? He clasped his hands tightly in front of him, face fixed and cold. It was difficult to tell himself that this was a bridge he could cross when he came to it, and that he did not have to consider the problem now. But if everything went well, they would be back in Nacogdoches within a month or so; and the problem may become urgent then, if LaVache had been right about the seriousness of the situation.

'I'll think about it when the time comes,' he said stiffly, knowing that the other was expecting some kind of an answer. He glanced up at the dark sky. Already, the fringes of the thin cloud were touching the edge of the moon. Soon it would be swallowed up.

Half an hour later, as he lay rolled in his blankets, a few yards from the crackling fire, listening to the faint rustle of the horse, hobbled in the brush, he tried to put his thoughts into some kind of order, thinking back over the past three years, since that day he had ridden into Nacogdoches with Henson and the wagon train. It seemed difficult to realise that so long a time had passed since then. Looking back on it, it seemed only a few weeks before. But a lot had happened in those three years, years which he had spent along the frontier in the company of Henri LaVache, riding old Indian trails, occasionally coming across odd little groups of men, Spaniards, Mexicans, Americans and Frenchmen, isolated from their fellow men, some looking for gold in the tall hills of the north, others merely content to get away from the rest of mankind, living by trapping, fighting when they were forced to, gaining a precarious sort of living from this hostile, inhospitable land. There had been the occasional brush with outlaws. Normally these men preferred to attack the rich wagon trains rolling west and ignored men such as himself. But there were vicious killers who shot on sight, took anything a man might have.

Now it seemed there might be a full-scale war between America and Mexico over the disputed territory of Tejas. Having driven the Spanish out, the Mexicans claimed dominion over the territory. But Mexico City was further from Tejas than the American frontier of Louisiana and there seemed little doubt that, if it came to a real showdown between the two countries, America would be able to put the larger force into the field and in the shorter time. The Mexican forces would be at a disadvantage. But that did not mean that any conquest of Tejas would be easy. There were undoubtedly those who believed that an American force had but to march into the territory, marshalling aid from the large number of American settlers there and the war would be won in a matter of weeks.

He exhaled slowly, shivered a little as the first drops of rain began to fall. They would be sleeping wet that night, he told himself. One of the horses snickered anxiously in the brush, possibly sensing the coming of rain and the sound jarred Bowie out of himself. He closed his eyes tightly, rolled over on to his side, pillowing his head on his arm.

By morning, the rain was gone. There was just the faintest indication of the storm in the east where a bar of dark cloud lay across the horizon, blotting out the light of the rising sun. But elsewhere, the sky was clear, right down to the rim of the flat land that lay to the south and west. There was a growing warmth in the air which brought some of the feeling back into Bowie's chilled limbs as he got to his feet, stirred the embers of the fire with his boot and tossed a large handful of branches on to it. Smoke began to lift as the flames tried to catch on to the damp wood, but ten minutes later, the fire had caught and there was the smell of roasting flesh and hot coffee in the still air.

Bowie ate hungrily, then rolled up his blanket, carried it to the waiting horse and strapped it securely across the back of the saddle. Ahead of them, the timber stretched clear up the side of the hill, all the way to the crest. He guessed that it continued for a long way down the far side too. It was not going to be easy finding a trail through there, he reflected.

When they rode out of camp, Aldred rode with him, while LaVache and Cain turned towards the western slope of the hills. Bowie watched them out of sight as they turned in among the steeply-rising rocks, then turned to face the tricky trail that wound along an out-thrusting ledge of rock in front of them, angling sharply into the timberline. They crossed a narrow gravel ford, reached higher, more dangerous ground and made slow progress. Once they reached the trees, they travelled without haste, giving their mounts time to blow. After the first quick rise, the hills began to break open into long, sloping benches of land where short-grass patches lay between the tall green tree masses and the going was a little easier.

Noon found them high on the slope in a small clearing, a place of tumbled rocks and thorn bushes. They did not build a fire here, but ate the long strips of meat they had brought in their pouches, cold. They were not far from the summit plateau now but above them the country roughened and it seemed that the pines turned smaller and ravines began to come down from the top. They would have to hold as close to the ridges as possible, then drop into the ravines, cross over and climb up to the next ridge, thereby working their way to the crest before moving on down the far side.

Bowie stretched himself and tightened the cinch under his mount's belly, checking his saddle roll. Aldred did the same, glanced up. 'We may run into bears here,' he said tightly. 'Some tracks yonder on the edge of the brush.'

'I noticed 'em,' Bowie nodded. He swung up into his saddle, held the reins loosely in his hands, waited for Aldred to mount up. There was a worried look on the

Bowie of the Alamo

other's face. Certainly bears could be unpredictable creatures. If a man made a mistake and simply wounded one, he could find himself face to face with one of the most fearsome creatures on God's earth.

They swung up into the trees, passed through them into more open, rock-strewn country. Their mounts picked their way forward carefully, moving over some of the roughest ground that Bowie had ever encountered. From down below, where they had made their camp the previous night, there had been no indication of this type of terrain. In places, they were forced to dismount and lead their horses, breaking forward through thickly-tangled vine and circling great masses of rock and sandstone, skirting long logs which lay across the rough trail.

This was the way of it for close on an hour, gradually working their way up the slope of the tall hill. The horses moved patiently with them, not liking this type of ground, but content to move forward. Presently, they came to a long wrinkle of ground that led upward, providing precarious footing, but evidently the only way up at that point. Bowie gave the steep-sided glen a cautious, all-embracing look, then turned to Aldred.

'We'll have to move up here,' he said tightly. 'It would take far too long to try to swing around it. Once we get to the top, the goin' should be easier . . .'

Aldred gave a quick nod. He paused for a moment, then began to edge his way forward. Bowie waited until the other had moved out of sight around a bend in the wrinkle, then put his mount to the steep upgrade. In places, he was forced to haul the bay over rough stretches of ground, shuffling his feet forward an inch at a time. At the top of the wrinkle, he sat for a moment on the wide ledge, drawing a long breath into his lungs, arms and elbows aching from the strain. Aldred was somewhere in the brush a few yards away. Bowie could hear him crashing through the undergrowth, circling around the more densely-populated stretch of the timber.

Five minutes passed. He could no longer hear the other

moving around and there was a deep silence over everything; a silence that was broken a moment later by the sudden shout from the timber and the savage roar, frightening and yet oddly familiar. Swiftly, Bowie came to his feet, releasing his hold on the reins. The horse shied away from him as he pulled the pistol from his belt and ran into the brush towards the sound. There was a harsh scream from almost directly ahead of him, a terrible sound that rang in his ears as he plunged forward.

The trail formed by Aldred, marked by broken branches was clearly visible. He turned a corner, thrust his way through thorn, ignoring the cuts across the backs of his hands and his face. The yelling had stopped but the crashing in the brush continued. Then, parting one of the bushes, he moved out into a small clearing. Aldred's horse was nowhere to be seen, had clearly been stampeded into the brush. Aldred was lying on the ground in the centre of the clearing, the huge bear standing over him, a menacing figure that turned, snarling savagely as Bowie stepped into the clearing.

Without pausing to think, he levelled the pistol and pulled the trigger, but even as he did so, the creature moved away from the prone body in the clearing, was moving towards him. He knew that the ball had hit the animal, but it had not struck it in a vital spot. Roaring savagely with pain, the bear lumbered forward, forelegs wide. There was no chance to turn and run, time only to face up to the enraged animal. Even as the bear struck him with all of its weight, his right hand caught at the hilt of the knife in his belt and tore it loose, fingers tightening around it.

The foetid stench of the animal's hot breath was on his face and he could feel his spine bending under the tremendous pressure. The snapping jaws were less than an inch from his face as he struck with all his force, feeling blood pour warmly over his hand and wrist as the knife went into the bear's shaggy coat. The bear gave a mad bellow of rage and its head went down, fangs glittering whitely in its head. Sucking air down into his tortured lungs, Bowie forced himself to hold on to his buckling consciousness, knowing that once he gave in, he was finished. The animal had been wounded, but was still dangerous. Again, the blade drew blood, but Bowie felt himself being drawn forward into those monstrous arms. Again and again, the knife ripped at flesh and bone and sinew, but still the animal squeezed. Bowie felt his ribs bending under the tremendous pressure that was being exerted on his body.

With a tremendous effort, he managed to tear his right arm loose. Now he had more room to swing the knife. Plunging it again and again into the animal's neck, he gritted his teeth against the pain in his chest. He could not hold on much longer. Already, there was a roaring in his ears that blotted out everything else and a red haze that danced in front of his straining vision.

Then, almost before he was aware of it, the animal's hold on him loosened. Sobbing air into his lungs, he staggered back, leaning his shoulders against the trunk of one of the trees behind him, shaking his head in an effort to clear it, every breath he took a stab of agony in his bruised and crushed body.

The bear was mortally wounded now. For a moment it stood swaying, forepaws weaving in front of its face. Then it collapsed at his feet and lay still. How long he stood there, forcing the strength back into his body, conscious of the deep scratches on his face and upper body, the blood flowing freely from them, staining his shirt. Slowly, his vision righted. He went to where Aldred lay and turned the other over, feeling for the pulse. He could detect nothing and the white face, eyes open and staring, told its own tale. He must have died almost at once. He made his way back, out of the clearing, past the dead body of the bear, down the slope to where his own mount stood waiting on the edge of the deep chute in the rocks. Leading it forward, he retraced his steps, moved around the clearing, eyes and ears alert. That bear might have a mate close by and he felt in no condition to battle another enraged animal such as the one he had just killed.

Progress was slow and difficult for the rest of the day. He reached the top of the hill shortly before nightfall, debated whether to make camp among the trees after the events of the day, then decided against it, and went on through the early part of the night, making his way downgrade. There was undoubtedly a better way of getting off the hills than this. Possibly LaVache and Cain had found it further to his left. As it was, he was forced to pause on several occasions when the trees dribbled out and the ground underfoot became little more than rock and earth, with some vegetation clinging precariously to it. There was no trail. He had to make his way forward in the darkness, before the moon came up shortly after midnight. The wounds in his body were beginning to ache intolerably now and a stab of pain went through him with every breath he sucked down into his lungs. The loss of blood had weakened him, but somehow, he forced himself to keep moving. Now and again, the horse faltered, slowed its pace almost to a crawl, then increased its gait for a little while as he touched spurs to its flanks. The horse was both tired and doubtful of this ground underfoot and in places, what little pathway there was pitched steeply downward, often vanishing into the darkness or pitch-black moon-thrown shadows that lay across it.

Then he moved into the vast shadow thrown by the bulk of the hill itself and he realised that he was moving blind. Now, he was forced to give up, to stop. He did not light a fire. Coffee could wait that night. There were less than five hours to dawn and he crawled into a tangle of vine, beating with a stick to scare off any snakes that might have taken cover there. The bay he had tethered to a stake, loosened off the rope so that it might chew the coarse grass.

In the morning, before the sun came up, he finished off the dried meat in his saddlebag, washed it down with water from a nearby stream and continued on down the slope of the hill. He did not meet up with the others until after midday, finding them on a wide, open stretch of ground where they had already made camp.

He saw the sudden gust of expression that passed over the Frenchman's face as he rode up to them alone. Before the other could speak, he said tightly: 'Aldred was killed back there on the hill by a bear. I couldn't get to him in time. He must've died almost at once, without a chance to defend himself. I wounded it with my pistol, then it attacked me. I guess I was lucky to get away with my life.'

'And the bear?' asked the other in a soft tone.

'I killed it with a knife,' said Bowie flatly. He shrugged his shoulders, grimaced a little as the wounds opened again, staining his shirt a bright red.

'You'd better wash those wounds of yours, *mon ami*,' said the other, turning back to the fire. 'If you don't, there could be infection.'

Bowie went over to the stream fifty yards away and bathed his wounds. The cold water stung the deep cuts where the bear's claws had raked across his flesh, but gradually the pain in them went away. The bleeding stopped. He pulled on his shirt again, went back to the camp. The coffee tasted better than anything he had drunk before and he drank it slowly, feeling the warmth and strength flow back into his body.

5
NACOGDOCHES

It was high noon in Nacogdoches as James Bowie sat at the table in the small cantina. The bottle in front of him was half empty now. Across the table, Fallon drummed nervously on the table top with his fingers. His eyes were sharp, his face lined with worry.

'I realise that it's three years since we last met, and you've been working for the Mexican Government up to the north, but things here have changed a lot since then.'

'How?' asked Bowie tightly. He gulped down the liquor in the glass. It hit the back of his throat, hot and raw.

'We've got to fight now, if we want to hold on to the land we have. We're being hounded at every turn. They tax us to the hilt, then demand some of our grain. If we refuse to pay, they send the soldiers, threaten to turn us out of the country. We've paid in full for that land and here we stay.' There was a vehemence in his voice which Bowie had not known before, when they had blazed that trail across from New Orleans to Natchitoches and then on across the Sabine wilderness into Tejas.

'And you think that you have a chance, fighting trained soldiers?' Bowie stared at the other in amazement.

'It's the only chance we're ever goin' to get here,' muttered the other thinly. 'Believe me, we've all talked this over, discussed it every way, and this is the only way

Bowie of the Alamo

we'll ever get to live in peace. Turn out the Mexicans and make Tejas into an American State as Louisiana is.'

'There's a mighty big difference between Louisiana and Tejas,' said Bowie quietly. He poured more of the liquor into the glass in front of him, closed his fingers around it, but did not lift it from the table.

'I don't see where the difference is,' declared the other stubbornly. There was a hard set to the line of his jaw and a little muscle in his left cheek, just below the eye twitched uncontrollably. His fingers tightened themselves together, the knuckles standing out whitely under the tanned skin.

'Just that France was willing to relinquish her claim to Louisiana and the time was ripe for America to buy the land. There was no reason to fight for it. Here, it's different. Mexico will never let Tejas go without a fight. There's the difference, only you seem to be too blind to see it.'

Fallon hesitated, stared down at his hands for a long moment, then shook his head emphatically. 'You're wrong. It isn't like that at all. We know exactly what we'll be up against once we try to take over Tejas. First we'll have to take Nacogdoches and then march west and south. But there are men who will come in with us and we were hopin' that you might see your way to—' He broke off, his voice trailing away into an uneasy silence.

Bowie eyed him over the rim of his glass as he lifted it to his lips. There was a sudden coldness in his body. He remembered the Mexican soldiers he had seen in the streets of Nacogdoches, knew that they would be well armed, would shoot to kill if the order was given from Mexico City.

'You want me to join your forces,' he said harshly.

The other looked at him steadily before replying, then nodded. 'We want you to be a leader,' he murmured.

'You've got to go by the laws of Tejas, no matter what happens,' he said finally. 'The American Government knows that there are several thousand of us here on Mexican territory. If there is any hardship, then it's up to them to make sure that our rights as human beings, and American citizens, are not violated.'

'I knew you wouldn't see things as they really are,' declared the other thinly. 'You've been away from here for too long to know how things are. We are no longer American citizens. We had to take Mexican nationality once we arrived in Tejas. That was one of the conditions of getting a land grant from the Government.'

'And now you want to go back on that? Is that it?'

Fallon pressed his lips tightly together. 'I know that I'm not putting this too well. I'm sure if you were to come with me and talk with Henson and some of the others, they could make you understand things as they really are.'

Bowie sat quite still for a long moment. At the other side of the cantina, a man came in and began brushing the floor with a rush broom, humming softly under his breath as he worked. The air inside the place was hot and stifling in spite of that fact that there were no windows.

This, he told himself, was the problem that LaVache had mentioned that night on the trail to the north when they had talked over the uneasy situation in Tejas, and the inevitable showdown that was coming. Now he was face to face with it, sooner than he had expected. Now was the time when a man had to take sides, when he fought with his own countrymen or against them. It was a difficult decision for him to take at this time. He had been well received by the Mexicans when he had arrived, had always been on good terms with them. Yet he still regarded himself as an American; nothing could change that.

'Very well, I'll meet Henson,' he said roughly. 'Where is he?'

The relief on the other's face was so obvious that it was almost painful to watch it, the way his shoulders slumped fractionally and the fingers, tightly clasped together, relaxed. 'He's out of Nacogdoches, about twenty miles to the south-west. I'll take you there. I've got a wagon outside.'

The journey out to Henson's land was one of long,

dusty tracks which could not be called roads. The wagon was evidently some years old and it swayed and rattled from side to side, making it a most uncomfortable journey for Bowie who was used to riding horseback. Even then the dust that hung thickly in the air would have been choking and bitter, but on the flat wagon, it was ten times worse. It worked its way into the folds of his skin, under his shirt, mingling with the sweat that stood out on his body, so that every move he made chafed and abraded his flesh.

There was a small herd of cattle on the ranch that Henson had built for himself, and a tall windmill used for lifting the water from the artesian well in the middle of the courtyard in front of the house. Henson himself came out on to the long, low porch as they rode in, stood shading his eyes against the glare of the sun as he peered across at them. Then he stepped down from the porch and walked forward.

'Glad you decided to come, Bowie,' he said genially, grasping the other's hand and shaking it warmly. 'I wasn't sure whether you would. After I'd sent Fallon along into Nacogdoches, I thought maybe I ought to have gone myself, maybe he wouldn't be able to talk you around to our way of thinking.'

'He hasn't done that yet,' Bowie told the other as they went into the house. 'He told me plenty about high taxes and the authorities wanting to turn you off your land. But that seems a little hard for me to believe. I've always been on good terms with the Mexicans.'

The other looked hard at him, then gave a harsh smile, opened one of the doors and ushered him into the parlour.

'They won't bother men like you who work for them, opening up new frontiers. But the truth is that they're afraid of the rest of us. They know that we're growing at a rapid rate. Too quickly for their liking, that pretty soon we'll outnumber them and once that happens, we'll start demanding that Tejas joins America. They want to stop that from happening. And we can't afford to let them stop us.'

'Then you really mean to fight?'

'For the Lord's sake, Bowie, why not? We have the right to protect our own. This was Mexican land once, but now that we've bought it, I figure that it's American soil.'

'Didn't you and the others take an oath of allegiance to the Mexican Government when you came here? Wasn't that a condition of getting a land grant?'

'So we took an oath,' boomed the other loudly. 'But there's a limit to what a man can take. We've reached that limit now that they are starting to take all of our money, taxing us to the point where we have nothing left and then taking half of everything we produce.'

'If you try to fight, there's the chance that you'll lose everythin'.'

'We know that. We've gone into this carefully and we have no other choice open to us. But there are men moving across the border now, ready to join us.'

Bowie tightened his lips. What sort of men were these of which the other spoke so glibly? He could guess. Adventurers, men looking not only for excitement but for the chance to kill, and if they could do so in the name of patriotism, so much the better. It meant they would not have to face the consequences when all this was over. They would be looked upon as heroes in the battle for liberty, whereas most of them would be nothing more than cutthroats and outlaws, as bad as those who pillaged and plundered along the Sabine.

'And you want me to lead you against the Mexicans?'

'Yes. The men will follow you. Once we've taken Nacogdoches, I reckon we can hold it until others join us. It's a long way to Mexico City and news travels slowly in these parts.'

There had been fighting earlier. It had flared up at various places in Tejas since the Mexican Government had resorted to very restrictive measures, doing all they could to stop Anglo-American colonisation of the state and encouraging Mexican immigration, abolishing slavery,

Bowie of the Alamo

levying heavy duties on the colonists and establishing their military garrisons in all strategic positions.

The turning point had come when they had declared martial law in Tejas and attempted to disarm the colonists. Fighting had broken out at Velasco, Anahuac, Gonzales and other places where the colonists had openly resisted. Led by Ben Houston, these colonists, although honest men, had seen no future for Tejas except in the United States. The main body of Americans under Stephen Austin down on the Brazos accepted Mexican citizenship in good faith, but even they were now beginning to see that there was little real future for them as things stood.

It was into this confusion of elements that James Bowie was thrust in the early part of 1832. The Americans, forced by the train of events, were banding themselves together. Armed militiamen prepared to fight for Tejas.

Bowie's first meeting with most of these men came two weeks after his talk with Henson. There was the smell of whisky in the large room although all of the men there seemed on the surface to be sober. Most of them were strangers to Bowie, moustached and bearded, faces open and hard, the lined faces of men who knew what it was to work and who had clearly had their fair share of trouble. They squatted on their haunches, or leaned their backs against the stone walls. Many rifles were in evidence and every man carried a pistol, sometimes two, thrust into their belts. They needed only uniforms to be soldiers, he thought, as he let his gaze roam over them. A tall, thick-set man rose and came forward to meet him.

'Glad to have you with us, Bowie,' he said warmly. 'We need every man who can use a rifle and from what I've heard of your exploits, you certainly come into that category, possibly more so than most of us here.'

There was a faint ripple of good-natured laughter from the men nearby. The other led him forward. 'I'm in charge of this gatherin', Mister Bowie. The name is Ben Milam. I reckon you can guess why we're here. The Mexicans have sent a force north to drive us out of this country. We mean to stay here in spite of everything they do, and if we have to fight, then by God we'll fight.'

'Do you know how many soldiers they're sending against you?'

The other's smile was hard, but a little uncertain. 'We know very little,' he confessed. 'But we're damned sure that no Mexican is goin' to turn us off our land. We're all determined that Tejas is to become a part of the United States.'

'Then you'll declare war on Mexico, even though it's likely that you'll get no official backing from Washington?'

'If it comes to that, we will,' affirmed the other harshly. 'At the moment, there's no question of declaring war on Mexico. All we intend to do is to defend ourselves and our families.'

'But from what I've heard you mean to attack Nacogdoches.'

The other nodded. 'That's the first part of our plan. We mean to show these soldiers that we're a force to be reckoned with. Then perhaps they'll listen to us.'

'They'll never listen to you. This has to be a fight to the finish. You know that, don't you?' The other hesitated, then gave a quick nod of his head. 'They told me that you were a very shrewd man, Mister Bowie. I'm beginning to find that out for myself.'

'You know what you're goin' to start if you march on Nacogdoches?'

'Sure, we know. And we're prepared for it. Once we start, all of the other colonists will rise up to join us. Most of us figure that Mexico has no more claim to Tejas than Spain had and I didn't hear much shouting when the Spanish were driven out.'

'Could be that you're right,' Bowie agreed. Politics meant little to him.

'I know I'm right,' asserted the other. 'But be that as it may, we're here to discuss the details of the attack. We've got close on three hundred men and as far as we know, the Mexican garrison in Nacogdoches amounts to less than two hundred soldiers.'

Bowie nodded briefly. 'But don't forget that these men are trained soldiers. Two hundred of them are equal to three hundred of your men.'

'Very well. I accept that. We start on equal terms. But I doubt if they will be expecting us to attack them. In the past, we've mainly fought only to defend ourselves. They'll be expecting us to do the same thing again, but this time, we mean to carry the attack to them. That way, we get the advantage of surprise.'

'You know what the consequences can be if you're wrong.'

'I'm not wrong,' said the other quietly, but with a touch of confidence in his tone. 'We attack the day after tomorrow – in force.'

In the trees overlooking Nacogdoches, there were close on a hundred men. Bowie let his glance wander over the nearest of them. They were all armed, hard-faced men who would fight once the order was given. Through the trees, it was possible to pick out most of the houses and churches in the town. The heat head had lifted during the morning, until now it struck at them forcibly and oppressively, so that details in the distance shivered and shook as if they were looking at everything through a rippling film of water. The assault was to come from three sides and Henson with his men was to the north of the town while Milam was to the west. He and the men with him were to attack from the south. He wiped the sweat from his forehead, cursed a little under his breath at the heat. At least, his force would have the sun at their backs, making it more difficult for the defenders. Henson and the others would not be so fortunate.

The sun was strong on his shoulders now, burning through the rough cloth of his shirt. In the distances, white walls shimmered brilliantly. The town seemed quiet from that distance, but it was a deceptive quietness. Inwardly, Bowie felt the tension mounting, an electric tautness which flashed from one man to another, bringing up their heads sharply at every untoward movement or sound.

'Why don't they start?' asked one of the men harshly. He rubbed the back of his hand down one cheek, slapped at a mosquito.

Bowie glanced at him briefly. 'Milam'll give the signal when he's ready. Ain't no point in moving in half-cocked. This has got to be a planned attack. He's got to make sure every man is in position. Now, you all know what to do when we attack?'

They nodded their heads slowly. A few murmured in affirmation under their breaths, tightened their grips on the long-barrelled rifles. Powder horns were slung over their shoulders.

A musket banged loudly on the other side of Nacogdoches. The sound carried easily in the still air and Bowie felt a little shiver pass through him as he motioned to the men with him. That was the signal for the attack to begin. Getting to their feet, they advanced on the outskirts of the town. A ragged volley of rifle fire broke out while they were still some distance away, indicating that some of the men had got through into the streets and had engaged the Mexican troops there.

Shots came from the buildings directly in front of them as they moved forward. Although taken by surprise, the defenders of the town had quickly gathered their scattered wits. A few desultory shots came in their direction as they ran forward, but so far no one was hit. Bowie was glad that he knew the lay-out of the town at this point. He could guess where the Mexicans would be in force. Quickly, he motioned the men to follow him. A bullet kicked up a spurt of dust a few feet in front of him and he flinched momentarily.

Two soldiers were on their knees in the middle of the street, in full view of them as they raced forward, the men evidently reloading their rifles. Nearby, a woman was on her knees in the dust, crossing herself. Bowie gave her a swift glance, then ignored her. Bringing up his rifle, he took quick aim at one of the soldiers and squeezed the trigger, felt the recoil of the weapon, then saw the man reel back, his weapon falling from his fingers, the side of his neck bloody where the bullet had torn through the flesh. He uttered a shrill bleating cry, then fell on to his back and lay still. His companion glanced up. An expression of utter surprise gusted over his swarthy features. For a moment, he fumbled with the rifle in his hands, then evidently thought prudence the better part of valour, dropped the gun, pushed himself to his feet and turned to run. One of the men behind Bowie fired at that moment and the soldier pitched forward on to his face, arms outflung.

Someone grasped Bowie's shoulder and pointed. Bowie looked across the side street in the direction of the other's pointing finger. More troops were moving up into position, taking cover in the small chapel on the opposite side of the street. From there, they would be able to bring heavy fire to bear on them, while remaining under cover themselves. Swiftly, Bowie looked about him, motioned the men into the shelter of one of the nearby houses. A low stone wall ran alongside the garden, filled with palm and exotic plants. Scarlet flowers grew in profusion, but there was no time to appreciate the beauty of the scene. Already, bullets were hitting the wall, showering them with powdered stone, the harsh, shrieking wail of the bullets as they ricocheted off the wall sounding in their ears.

'Keep firing,' he called loudly as some of the men hesitated. From another part of town, the firing increased savagely in volume as more of the rebels moved in to the attack. Bowie tightened his lips, ducked his head as a bullet smashed into the wall within inches of his skull. A man close by yelled loudly and long, fell back with blood showing on his shirt. Another threw up his hands in front of his face, dropped without a sound.

Bowie sucked in a sharp breath. In spite of the protection afforded by the wall, they were too exposed and already it was apparent that several of the soldiers had made their way on to the flat roof of the chapel and were firing down on them. From there, it was possible for them to pick them off one by one. Glancing up, he caught a glimpse of the uniformed man who exposed himself for a brief moment on the level roof of the chapel, the rifle lifted to his shoulder. Whether the other was blinded by the glare of the sunlight falling directly into his eyes, or whether he had foolishly disregarded his obvious danger in the excitement of getting one of the rebels in his sights, it was impossible to tell; but he remained standing there in full view of Bowie for several seconds, long enough for the other to draw a bead on him and press the trigger. For a moment, it seemed as if the shot had missed. The man stood on the edge of the roof, still gripping the rifle, as if he were carved out of stone. Then he swayed drunkenly, arms falling to his sides, the rifle clattering down the wall of the building to crash into the street, a bare handful of seconds before his dead body followed it, turning over and over in the air before he hit the ground with a sickening thud, raising a little cloud of dust which settled only slowly around his inert body.

But although that man had been killed, there were a score more on the roof, keeping themselves out of sight except for the brief moments when they opened fire on the men in the garden. Sharply, Bowie called: 'We've got to take the chapel. It's our only chance. If we stay here we're finished.'

'That's madness,' protested the man lying next to him. Sweat lay on the other's face, trickling down his cheeks and into his eyes. 'We don't stand a chance. They can shoot every man down before we cross the street.'

'Not if we leave a handful of men behind here to give us covering fire until we reach the chapel.'

The other still looked dubious, but Bowie motioned six of the men to spread themselves out behind the wall, then rallied the others to him. 'When we reach the chapel, use your pistols, then your knives. There'll be no time to reload.'

There was a shot from the direction of the chapel. The bullet skimmed off the top of the wall, howled into the sunlit distance. Three soldiers appeared on the edge of the roof, began firing down on them as Bowie waved his arm, urging the men forward across the street. Behind them, the muskets banged as the others gave them covering fire and out of the corner of his eye, as he ran forward, feet kicking up the dry yellow dust, Bowie saw the men on the roof drop flat as bullets howled among them.

Breathing heavily, they reached the white wall of the chapel, pressed their bodies against it, feeling the stone hot under their hands, burning with the stored-up heat of the strong sun. Carlsen, tall and blond-haired, stepped suddenly out from the wall, pointed his pistol vertically into the air and pulled the trigger. There was a wild, fearful cry from almost directly over their heads and a man pitched from the roof to hit the street less than a yard from where they stood. Grinning viciously all over his face, Carlsen moved back to the wall, stood quite unconcernedly there and calmly reloaded the pistol. Inside the chapel, there was a confused shouting. The soldiers on the roof had seen what was happening, could guess at their next move and were yelling harshly down to their companions below.

'Inside!' called Bowie. In the cool shadows inside the building, three figures appeared through the inner door. There was a loud bang as one of the men behind Bowie fired. In the confined space, the shot sounded oddly loud, echoes shuddering through the building. One of the Mexicans staggered, then crumpled up, making curious gurgling sounds that were horrible to hear. The other two poised irresolute in the doorway, staring about them with wide eyes. One died as Bowie fired. The other turned to run, died instantly with Bowie's knife between his shoulder blades.

Moving forward swiftly, Bowie jerked the knife free, wiped the blade on the man's tunic, then moved towards the stairs leading up to the roof. There was the sudden clatter of feet moving down as he set his foot on the bottom-most step. Bowie pushed himself back against the wall, holding his breath, the broad-bladed knife gripped in his right hand. A shadow fell across the bend in the stone steps. One of the men from the roof came running down, holding his rifle in his hand, his face twisted into a grimace of fear. By the time he spotted Bowie standing there it was too late for him to stop himself. He attempted to bring up the rifle even as he was running down the steps, feet slithering on the smooth stone, mouth wide open, eyes staring. Even as he realised there was no chance to use the rifle, was on the point of swinging it in his hands as a club, Bowie stepped in under the blow. His knife slid between the other's ribs. The man coughed deep in his throat. His weight pulled the knife free as he fell forward, feet going from under him. He hit the floor at the bottom of the steps, lay still.

Bowie motioned the rest of the men up the steps. In single file, they raced up the narrow stone steps. At the top, one man reeled back as a musket banged. But the others ran on. Firing broke out on the roof as Bowie moved up after the others. The body of the man who had been killed lay slumped at the top of the steps where they opened out on to the roof. He did not pause to give it a second glance. It was clear from the wound that the man had died instantly. Inwardly, he felt a strange coldness as he moved out into the open. Was there really any sense in men dying and killing each other in this way; men who had everything to live for, wives, and families.

Pandemonium had broken out on the flat roof. The soldiers had been cornered on the far side, were now pinned between the men who had come up the steps and the others in the garden on the opposite side of the street. Bowie smiled grimly to himself as he crouched down. It was only a matter of time before this force of soldiers were killed or surrendered as soon as they realised that their position was utterly hopeless. Meanwhile, the firing that was going on throughout the rest of the town told him that the battle had flared up into a full-scale conflict.

Bowie of the Alamo

There was going to be no stopping the rebels now in spite of everything the Mexican forces could do.

Two of the soldiers had stationed themselves behind a tall stone pillar and were aiming and shooting steadily from their cover, hoping that some of their bullets might find their targets. Bowie chanced a quick look from the head of the stone steps. One soldier lay face-down less than three yards away in a pool of dark red. It was clear that the soldiers knew their position was hopeless, but they kept on firing, possibly in the hope that some reinforcement might manage to get to them before they were overrun. Crouching down low, Bowie gritted his teeth, kept a tight grip of his knife, checked the second pistol he carried in his belt, then crawled forward around the perimeter of the roof, hoping to take the men by surprise. When he reached the corner he found himself looking straight at a Mexican soldier, kneeling there, reloading the long-barrelled rifle. The man swivelled round; opening his mouth to yell a warning to his companions as he did so. There was no time for him to bring up the rifle, even if it were loaded. He made a wild grab for the pistol in his belt, but before his fingers could close about the smooth butt, the knife in Bowie's hand struck home. The man gasped, reeled back. A second quick thrust and the man died. Licking dry lips, Bowie turned to face the other man, then relaxed. He found himself staring down into wide-open eyes that looked up at him, but did not see.

Slowly, cautiously, he got to his feet, stood for a moment, drawing air down into his lungs, staring about him. There was no more firing around the chapel. For a moment, he stared down at the stained knife in his hand, then pushed it back into his belt. Two of the rebels came forward, stood beside him, chests heaving under their shirts. One man rubbed a bloodied hand over his temple, leaving a smear of red on his flesh. He stood resting his weight on his rifle.

'They're finished here,' he said roughly. His breath rasped harshly in and out of his throat.

'There are still many more of them left in Nacogdoches,' Bowie said thinly. He reloaded the two pistols, thrust them back into his belt. Firing continued down in the streets. During the whole of that long, hot, sultry afternoon, the fighting went on with the Mexicans holding out throughout the town. Here and there, small groups surrendered when it was clear that their position was hopeless. But most of them fought on, fought on into the dim twilight, now outnumbered.

Sporadic fighting went on for the next two days around Nacogdoches. The Mexican forces were not easily defeated. When it was finished, the Mexicans had withdrawn from the town, pulling out to the south.

Dust was a silver screen in the streets of Nacogdoches. Bowie shouldered his way through a group of men standing in the middle of the street and went into the small cantina on the far side. Ben Milam, seated with Henson at one of the round tables, motioned him across. There was a bottle of wine on the table and a fresh glass was brought for him. Sitting down, Bowie let his gaze run over the others. Milam was still the same, he reflected; but there was no doubt that Henson had changed a great deal since he had first known him. No longer was the other the simple farmer. He was a soldier, a man determined to fight for what he believed to be right. There was a look of assurance about him now that went well with his broad build and the flowing black beard.

'We'll have to be careful,' Milam said quietly. 'The Mexican Government are ready to send more soldiers to Nacogdoches and northern Tejas. They haven't given up this territory.'

'They won't try to take this land away from us,' muttered Henson harshly. He shook his head. 'We've beaten them. Don't you realise that?'

'No, my friend.' Milam gave the other a studying glance. 'They'll come back – and soon. And we must be ready to meet them. When they do come, they'll find facing them, not a rabble of farmers and adventurers, but a trained army. If the American Government in Washington refuses to help us take Tejas for them, then we must do it ourselves.'

Henson shrugged his shoulders. For a moment, there seemed to be some answer to that balanced in his mind, but he said nothing, poured some of the wine into his glass and drank it in one thirsty gulp, set the empty glass down on the table in front of him, fingers still curled around it.

'Are we strong enough to take on everything that Mexico can throw against us?' asked Bowie quietly.

'We must be,' said Milam passionately. 'If they defeat us now, it may be many years before we're ever strong enough again, if we ever are.' He gave Bowie a bright-sharp glance. 'Some of the men who are crossing the border, hoping to join our forces, I wish I could be as sure of them as I am of the settlers.' There was a worried note to his voice.

'You sound as though you don't trust 'em,' said Bowie softly.

'I don't. They're all men who're hungerin' for a fight and I reckon a lot of 'em don't really care which side they fight on. The one that pays the most, I guess, in many cases.'

'If they'll join us against the Mexicans, we'll take care of 'em once it's all over should they decide to turn lawless,' put in Henson thinly.

'It may not be as easy a thing to do as you seem to think,' said Milam. 'I've seen some of these men and a more vicious lot of cut-throats it's never been my lot to meet.'

'As bad as that,' murmured Bowie softly. His mind went back several years, to the days he had spent in Louisiana and he could guess at the other's worry. If men such as that joined their forces, initially to fight the Mexicans, and then to carve out an empire of lawlessness for themselves, Tejas would not be a state worth living in as far as honest men and women were concerned. Always, whenever a new country was being colonised, the bad came in with the good and at first, it was difficult to distinguish between the two.

'Worse, I'm afraid. We have very little choice in the matter. Without these men we will be defeated once the Mexican Army arrives. If we accept their help, we may be fashioning a millstone for our own necks.'

Bowie nodded. He could guess at the thoughts which must have been going through the other's mind at that moment. He wondered how the other got his information concerning the Mexican troop movements. Did Milam have spies in Mexico City or was that just an intuitive guess, possibly very close to the truth? It did not seem possible that there could be men in Mexico City supplying him with this sort of information – and yet Bowie could not help remembering the days when the pirate gangs along the Mississippi and the outlaw bands along the Natchez Trace had men in New Orleans, spying on the wagon trains that moved out, heading west. The same sort of thing might apply here.

'Just what is it that you're afraid of, Milam?' asked Henson roughly. It was clear he had drunk a little more of the wine than was good for him and it had loosened his tongue.

'Afraid of?' The other glanced up and for a moment, there was a look of surprise on his face. Then his lips parted in a faint smile. 'I think,' he said, 'that you know the Mexicans as well as I do. Sure, we fought them here a couple of years ago, but a lot of things have happened since then. Fighting has broken out at other places, and we haven't always been the victors. They foresaw that something like this might happen and that's the reason they set up their chain of military posts, so that they could send a strong force of their men to virtually any part of the country, quickly. Our ability to do that is limited.'

Bowie nodded. Inwardly, he too, was a little worried. Their victory at Nacogdoches had not been as decisive as he would have liked, and that would have changed the situation quite appreciably, might even have forced the Mexicans to have pulled out all of their forces from Tejas. But now there was only one thing sure – there would be more trouble – bad trouble. When, he didn't know. Perhaps even Milam was unsure of when and where the Mexicans would strike again, or how strong they would be when they did. He emptied his glass and set it down.

Half an hour later, he went out into the warm sunlight. The town was quiet and there was little to show that it had changed at all during the past three years. But there had been changes there. The American population were now more firmly in control than ever before. True there were still Mexicans there, some Spaniards and Frenchmen, but it was the Americans who ruled here in Nacogdoches. How long that situation would last, was problematical. No one knew what the Mexican Government intended to do now – although Milam had probably guessed right. Drawing in a deep breath, Bowie looked about him and for the first time, he seemed to be seeing the place with new eyes. When he had first moved into Tejas, there had been only a few dim lights of civilisation burning in the great dark wilderness of this territory and Nacogdoches had been one of them. But now they were hard at work opening up this vast country. Soon, there would be as many men and women here as in Louisiana, and as many cities too, places such as New Orleans and Natches. If this land was of little use for farming, then they could breed cattle here, millions of cattle, feeding on the vast grasslands of Tejas.

For the first time, too, the full immensity of what they were doing at that time came to him. If – and when – they did have to fight, he did not doubt that it would all be worthwhile. There were always men who were willing to fight and die for a dream, provided it was big enough – and no one could deny that the state of Tejas was big enough for any man.

There had been moments in the past when he had

wondered whether he was doing the right thing, fighting against the Mexicans who had always treated him fairly and well. Now he was quite convinced that he was doing the only thing possible for him. It was right that Tejas should become a part of the United States. Only by doing so, could it become great. A wry smile played on his lips for a moment as that thought passed through his mind. How many of the men now willing to fight for Tejas thought that way? he wondered.

6
RIDING HIGH

The raw, yellow, naked country around Nacogdoches was barren even compared with certain stretches of Louisiana. Wide sandy distances that were rimmed by the rising, flat-topped mesas, great upthrusting pieces of land on which the clouds sometimes hung, white and feathery. But there were other times when they glowed redly in the harsh, brilliant glare of the sunlight, or eerily with the whiteness of the moon. Along the bottom of the narrow valley which ran between two of these massive outcrops of sandstones, a river had once run; but now there was nothing but the dried-out watercourse, cracked soil from which all of the moisture had long been sucked avidly by the heat. The only visible stretch of green lay in the distance, where some of the immigrants had succeeded in finding a small well which they used to irrigate the land, growing sparse vegetable crops, keeping a few animals.

But the men on the wide, heat-soaked ledge of the mesa had no eyes for this. They had been there for close on two days now and their food and water were both low. Grumbling, they tried to find some shade from the pitiless glare of the sun; but once it had worked its way around to the south, there was no place where they could go to escape the terrible heat and light.

Bowie squatted a little distance from the others, staring out across the wide plain that lay below them. From their vantage point, it was possible to see for a great many miles in virtually every direction, out to where the smooth and flat horizons shivered and twisted behind the curtain of heat haze. Dust devils cavorted across the plain, spinning clouds of sand grains, lifted by the freakish winds which often sprang up without warning.

Bowie emerged from his daydream as Fallon edged forward, dropped down limply beside him and said in a harsh, rasping tone: 'Don't you think we've been here on this ledge of hell long enough, Jim? Sure they were so damned positive that the Mexicans would be sending a column of their men through this way, but we've seen neither hair nor hide of 'em. I say they ain't coming this way, if they're headin' this way at all.'

'Milam was sure,' said Bowie flatly. He didn't like the task of waiting here in the glaring day heat and the terrible cold of the night any more than the others did, but it was important that this Mexican column should be stopped before it got through to the town and this was the only place where they stood a chance of taking the enemy by surprise. From here, they could fire down on the column with little risk of being shot themselves. It was an old Indian trick and he felt certain it would work this time. The Mexicans had had very little trouble with the Indian nations in Tejas, during the whole of the time they had been in possession of the country and they would have had very little experience of anything quite like this. It was his belief, that they would come marching through this valley without paying any heed to what lay in wait for them on the rugged slopes of the mesas.

'Damn Milam,' spat Fallon tautly. 'I notice that he ain't here with the rest of us. He'll be takin' it easy in one of the cantinas, drinking his fill, while we stay and burn out here, with hardly enough water to last us back into town, even if we was to set off right this minute.'

'We stay here,' said Bowie harshly. He pushed himself to his feet and brushed away the sweat that trickled down his forehead, into his eyes, half blinding him. 'You and the others call yourselves soldiers. Then you'll have to learn to obey orders whether you like 'em or not.'

He saw the look that passed over the other's face, saw the indecision in the man's eyes. It was plain that Fallon had always considered himself to be a tough one, ready to answer any challenge made to him, or his manhood. But at heart, he was still a farmer, drawn into this quarrel perhaps through no fault of his own. He knew that the eyes of the rest of the men were on him, watching to see how this battle of wills would go. All of the men, Bowie felt sure, wanted to leave this hell place, ride back and tell Milam that the Mexicans had not arrived, had possibly taken some other trail, or that his information regarding their movements had been false; anything to get away from here.

Fallon slitted his eyes and set his lips into a tight line. His big fists clenched and unclenched by his sides. Bowie stared at him steadily, waiting for the other to lower his gaze. For almost a minute, Fallon nursed his resentment in silence, then he said throatily, 'The rest of the men are at the back of me on this, Bowie. We don't aim to spend much longer here waiting for a Mex column that maybe ain't comin' this way at all.'

'You're bluffin', Fallon,' said Bowie tautly. 'You reckon that you're the man to give the orders here. Since when were you put in charge of this group? I say what we do and what we don't do.'

'Not any longer,' roared the other savagely. 'For two days now, we've endured this hell. Two days on short rations and not enough water to keep a dog alive, let alone a man. And now you're tellin' us to stay here until we either die of the heat or thirst.'

Bowie grinned viciously. In spite of the other's talk, now that he stood before an actual challenge, the reality of it stiffened him. He had a belief in himself, blown up by the fact that he felt certain the men would back him if he made a move; yet all of this began to crumble slowly before Bowie's steady and unblinking gaze. Bowie saw the man's courage begin to sag, saw the fractional droop of his shoulders as his pride wavered back and forth, unequal to the issue at hand. Then, abruptly, the other dropped his gaze, turned his head sharply to cover his weakness, and stared at the rest of the men, lying or squatting on the hot rock.

'Are you goin' to sit there and let him kill us? Don't you see what he's doin'? He means to keep us here until he's sure that the Mexs don't turn up, whether it kills any of us or not. He isn't concerned about us, only about carryin' out orders.'

Some of the men muttered under their breaths, and Bowie saw their red-rimmed eyes flick in his direction. With an effort, he got to his feet and it was at that moment that Fallon made his move. He had clearly been waiting for a moment such as this when he hoped to catch Bowie off his guard. Swinging round, he flung out his arms, caught them tightly around the other's ankles and threw all of his weight forward. It was impossible for Bowie to keep his balance under the sudden and unexpected attack. He went down on his back, the impact knocking all of the air from his lungs. The back of his skull struck an upthrusting stone and for a moment, consciousness threatened to leave him. Desperately, he fought to hold on to his senses. Fallon fought with the fury and strength of a man desperately afraid, and hurt by the blow to his pride.

Sucking air down into his lungs, Bowie forced himself over on one side, twisting up one leg as the other tried to kick him in the stomach. The heavy boot caught him on the shin and a vicious stab of pain lanced through him.

Fallon was muttering hoarsely under his breath as he tried to wriggle on top of Bowie, hoping to use his full weight to hold him down while he got a strangle hold on him.

'Damn you, Bowie, you ain't keepin' me here to die,' he kept repeating through tightly clenched teeth, eyes half closed.

Bowie took more bruising punishment on his shin as he fought to throw the other off. Fallon lunged for his throat, features twisted like those of a crazy man. But the other was panicking, possibly realising that he had made a mistake, that his chances of success were fast slipping away from him. Bowie made his body go limp for a brief moment then, as the other suddenly relaxed his pressure, stabbed up with quick, short jabs to the man's face. He could not get all of his force and weight behind the blows, but they landed solidly on Fallon's face, sending his head jerking back on his neck. Blood spurted from his nose and there was a red weal above his left eye as Bowie continued to hammer several blows home.

With a choked curse, Fallon reeled away, spitting out several teeth from his smashed mouth. Bowie followed him, lunging to his feet, slipping a little to one side as the other tried to rush forward and force him off the edge of the ledge, sending his body down to mangled death on to the rocky valley floor a couple of hundred feet below.

Now that he had both arms free and the wavering red haze was gone from in front of his vision, Bowie was able to square up to the other, to see him clearly. The man's face was a mess of blood. It trickled from the cut over his eye and ran down from his nose, getting into his mouth as he tried to stand upright, blinking his eyes several times as if he were having difficulty seeing properly. Fallon hesitated for a moment, then rushed forward, arms flailing. Bowie waited, knowing that he had the other now, that Fallon was finished.

Ducking under the wildly swinging arms, Bowie felt a fist graze his ear. Then he sent a couple of hard-fisted punches into the man's chest, heard the breath whoosh from his lungs as the blow threatened to capsize the other's ribs. Fallon grunted and stopped dead in his tracks. His arms fell limply to his sides and he stood swaying, eyes half closed. He did not seem to know where he was as Bowie hammered his right fist on to the side of the other's head. Fallon went down on to his back as if he had been pole-axed. He lay still, out cold, his breathing heavy, bubbling through the blood in his mouth.

Drawing himself up to his full height, still feeling some of the anger in him, Bowie glared at the rest of the men. 'Anyone else got ideas like his?' he asked tightly.

No one said anything, most of them looking away. A few stared down at Fallon's unconscious body and he thought he saw an expression of contempt in their eyes. For a moment, he stood there, then he went over and dragged Fallon away from the rim of the ledge.

The sun lifted higher into the cloudless heavens and the heat head continued to grow more intense. There was little talk from the men as they sat huddled together on the ledge. It was almost impossible now to look down into the valley below. The terrible waves of heat and light, reflected from the dusty sand blinded them, made it difficult to stare at the ground for more than a few seconds. Bowie sat with his back and shoulders against the rock, at a point where the ledge was less than three feet wide, where he could look down to the valley without moving his position if he wished to do so. There was no sense of time now. The minutes dragged themselves by into a sun-blinding, nerve-stretching torture which transcended anything that Bowie had experienced before.

He wiped the sweat from his forehead, touched the back of his skull gingerly with his fingertips, feeling the place where it had crashed on to the rocky ledge. There was no bleeding, but the spot was sore and tender to the touch. A few feet away, Fallon suddenly moaned, moved his head, then rolled over on to his side and tried to push himself upright. His head hung between his arms and he seemed to have difficulty in drawing air down into his chest. Then he lifted his head and stared across at Bowie, tried to swallow. A look of agony flashed over his features as he moved his bruised lips. One hand went up to his face and he felt the deep cut over his eye and the bloodied nose. With an effort, he sat back on his haunches, silent for a long moment as he felt for any further damage.

Bowie watched him closely for a long moment, then nodded his head slightly. There would be no further trouble from the other, he decided. Fallon had had enough. He had found himself face to face with his own private ruin. His inward admiration for himself had vanished suddenly, his courage had gone. He had failed himself and his face revealed the inner sickness of it.

The long, heat-filled afternoon passed painfully slowly. Bowie took several small sips of the water in his canteen, rolled the liquid around his mouth before swallowing it, but by now his mouth was so parched that it seemed to absorb all of the water before it got a chance to reach his throat. He was nursing a very odd feeling and nothing seemed to help. This mood, irritable and unsatisfied, a formless feeling that perhaps Fallon and the other men had been right in their supposition, that the Mexicans would not send a force through the valley to attack the settlers in the town, grew stronger as the sun passed beyond its zenith and began to lower towards the western horizons. Within a few hours, the heat would leave the air, but it would not bring much relief for them. There would be a brief moment while the air held a residual warmth left over from the scorching heat of the day, but that moment would soon pass and the terrible, intense cold of the night would freeze the blood in their veins, numbing their limbs.

He sat loose in his joints, kneaded the muscles at the back of his neck, then ran a hand over the hot rock under him, aware of the solidity of it. The solidity of it helped him a little in a strangely indefinable way. It seemed to be the only solidity anywhere and that was a queer thing to think about. In the old days, long before this trouble had flared up, he had been able to travel carefree, anywhere he wished and the days had run on in their own way, hot or cold, wet or dry and everything had been fun with a sense of achievement, every feeling good and strong on his nerves. The past meant nothing then and the future was merely something still to come; only the immediate present mattered. Now all of that had been altered. The future was a pressing and demanding thing, bringing its fear and worries with it. Coming events were casting their shadows ahead of them, affecting everyone strongly. He let his weight settle heavier on his haunches, lifted his head and stared out into the vast and stretching wilderness that lay in front of them, out to the wide and limitless horizons, where the desert lay like one single melted surface.

As far as the eye could see, nothing seemed to move. Leaning back, he tried to reach out with his thoughts to the old times, but could find nothing there. He sighed, reached for the canteen lying on the rocks beside him, made to pull out the cork with his teeth, then stopped with the canteen halfway to his lips. Out there to the southwest, there was something moving. Too far away for anything to be picked out individually, yet there was no mistaking that column of figures as they came closer over the desert.

He lurched swiftly to his feet, saw out of the corner of his eye, the rest of the men turn their heads in his direction. Even Fallon had stopped his mumbling and was staring at him.

Bowie pointed, out into the sunlight. 'There they are,' he said hoarsely. 'The Mexican column and they're headed this way. If they keep up that pace, they ought to be here before dark.'

The men scrambled to their feet. All of their previous apathy seemed forgotten now. A heavy man said: 'I thought you were wrong, Jim. How many do you reckon there are?'

'Does it matter,' growled another man thickly. 'We can take 'em from here, however many there are.' He reached out, grabbed his rifle and checked his powder horn.

The land was deceptive. It was soon obvious that the column was further away than they had seemed, the clear desert air making details sharper, more magnified than normal. An hour passed. Now it was possible to confirm that this was a military column. It was not as large as Bowie had been expecting and it came to him then that perhaps the Mexican commander had been a little more shrewd than they had given him credit for, and had split his forces, sending one column across the desert from the south-west, while the other circled around to come upon the settlers from the north. If that was indeed the case, then Milam and his force would have to take care of the other column, while they attacked this one. He threw a quick glance at the sky. The sun was still dipping towards the western horizon, but it would soon be gone. The chances were that the enemy would camp in the valley below if darkness fell by the time they reached it.

All of the men were alert now. The slanting rays of the sinking sun glanced off the tops of the mesas and turned the stretching desert into a land of contrasts. Most of it lay in deep shadows, and here and there, deep gullies slashed the red and yellow with slits of midnight shadow. But the mesas themselves still gleamed brightly as they caught the sunlight.

'I figure they'll make camp here,' Fallon said gruffly. He spoke slowly through his broken teeth and swollen lips. He seemed to have forgotten the fight with Bowie for the moment, everything swallowed in the need to be ready to destroy these men who were riding towards them.

'We'll wait until they're ready to make camp and then attack,' Bowie said loudly, so that every man could hear.

Fallon looked up quickly. 'You think that's wise,' he muttered. 'Why don't we wait until they're asleep? They'll only have a handful of guards and we could deal with those.'

'You think we're outlaws on the Natchez Trace,' Bowie said fiercely. 'Those men down there aren't farmers. They're soldiers. We don't have any chance of taking their sentries by surprise. If we strike when they're dismounted and pitching camp, we have the best chance of surprising them.'

Fallon made as if to protest further, then clearly thought better of it and closed his mouth tightly, turned away sullenly and picked up his rifle. The Mexicans were close against the edge of the other mesa, directly opposite them and on the far side of the narrow valley. Soon, they would work their way into it, move into the dark shadow thrown by the looming bulk of the mesa.

Bowie counted more than three score men, moving in single file except where three rode abreast at the head of the column. They were obviously wary, expecting trouble here if it was to come anywhere along the trail. The land suddenly crowded in on them at this point and it was a place where settlers could swoop down without warning and attack from close quarters. The men moved with caution and although they were still at a considerable distance, he could make out their uniforms, and the fact that the man in the lead was an officer. Bowie pulled his rifle towards him, steadying the barrel on an upthrusting rock, drew a thoughtful sight on the officer. In another five minutes, the whole outfit would have ridden into the narrow, steep-sided valley and it would be then that they would decide whether to camp there or ride on through the night. If they decided to keep on riding, it was essential that he and his men should open fire before the others rode out into the open again. He heard a scrape behind him, and two of the men came forward, crouching low. There was little chance of being seen from the valley, but with the sunlight still touching the rocks about them, there was no point in taking unnecessary risks.

'Looks as though they mean to ride on right through,' growled one of the men gruffly. He lifted his rifle carefully, holding it balanced in his hands.

'No. They're stopping,' muttered Bowie. Down below, the officer in the lead had wheeled his mount and was signalling the men to stop. Slowly, the column came to a standstill. Another few moments, then the commander dismounted, moved forward to the nearer entrance of the valley and stepped out into the open, peering about him closely, warily.

The man next to Bowie laughed harshly. 'Reckon he isn't sure,' he said with a trace of grim, sardonic amusement in his voice.

'Be ready to open fire as soon as I give the word,' Bowie

said, almost as if he had not heard what the other had said.

The men nodded, lay prone on the still-warm rock, sighting along their rifles, their faces hard, caked with dust and sweat. Bowie lowered his rifle on the officer, finger tight on the trigger. With that man dead, the column would be temporarily leaderless and that was what he wanted. The officer, if still alive once the attack began, might pause to consider the position, might urge his men back on to their mounts, ride out into the open where they were superior. If he were killed at once, the others may hesitate.

He waited patiently until the officer turned and made his way slowly back to the others, until the order had been given to dismount. Then he sighted once more on the short man who stood a little distance away from the rest of the men, hesitated for the barest fraction of a second before pressing the trigger. The savage bark of the rifle shattered the silence into a thousand screaming pieces. Down below, the officer had crumpled to the ground, lay still. One of the horses, terrified by the sudden shot broke free of the man holding the reins, lashed forward, its hooves striking the body of the officer underfoot, hammering it into the ground. The rest of the men, ignoring the horses, scattered for the loose rocks and boulders on either side of the valley, crouching down out of sight.

A rattle of rifle fire broke out from all the way along the ledge. There was little cover in the valley and more of the soldiers died. The horses, with no restraining hands on the reins, stampeded at the racket, raced for the opening of the valley and ran into the desert beyond.

'We've got them pinned down now,' yelled one of the men gruffly. Squatting back, he reloaded the rifle.

Down below, men cowered under the savage lash of bullets. Some tried to fire up at the figures on the ledge, but to do so they were forced to stand out in the open and expose themselves to the accurate fire from above. Bowie threw a quick look about him. It would be possible, once darkness fell, for the trapped soldiers to move out of the valley without being seen. There would be no moon that night. He reached a sudden decision.

There was a trace of steely hardness in his voice as he snapped: 'Fallon! Take half a dozen men with you and block off the far exit of the valley. Conlan, you do the same with this end. I don't want any of 'em slipping through my fingers after dark.'

The men moved away along the ledge in either direction, making scarcely any sound. There were no tell-tale movements down below and he guessed that the men had gone under cover now, possibly knowing that their only chance of escape from this trap lay with the coming of night. Bowie smiled grimly to himself. Well, he and the men with him could outwait them. He settled back against the smooth rock, tried to ease his body into a more comfortable position, but it was not easy. Stones and boulders seemed to be everywhere, grinding into his body until it was a mass of bruises and torn, lacerated flesh. There was no point in wasting precious ammunition and powder now, shooting at shadows. The little movements down below were not things a man could use as a target. Besides, he told himself fiercely, there was no hurry. Out here, in this land of renegades and settlers, it was the ways of the animal that counted, the fundamental instincts of planning ahead and working out what your enemy meant to do. The enemy's biggest mistake had been riding into that valley without sending in scouts first. Here, the settlers knew every trick there was and had no scruples about using them.

He looked up at the darkening sky. The sun had dropped behind the horizon with a vivid red glow, like some vast explosion far down over the rim of the world. Already, the first stars were beginning to show in the east and the air had lost a lot of its heat. He felt the coolness flow against his face, momentarily fresh and like a balm on his skin. Settling the rifle athwart his right knee, he waited for the enemy to make their move. His heart was beating in long, steady strokes now and his breathing was back to normal.

Once darkness fell and the intense cold came seeping up from the ground, Bowie knew that it would be extremely easy for their eyes to deceive them in that shifting, shadow-filled blackness. Several times, he thought he detected movement in the valley and jerked himself to his feet, fingers closing around the butt of the rifle. But although he strained his eyes and ears, he could pick out nothing definite. He sank back onto the rocks. Around him, the men were still awake. Their thirst would, he knew, keep them awake.

'Somebody movin' yonder,' croaked the man nearest him. The other pointed a finger.

'You sure?' Bowie could see nothing in the blackness. Then, at the corner of his vision, he made out the sudden movement, down among the tumbled boulders at the far side of the valley. He stiffened abruptly, gave a quick nod to indicate that he had spotted them. 'Let's hope that Fallon and his men are awake and ready for them,' he grunted. 'They all seem to be movin' in that direction.'

Lifting his rifle, he aimed it at one of the shadows, pressed the trigger and sent sound bucketing across the narrow valley. The echoes of the single shot bounced off the far walls of the opposite mesa and were reflected back into the valley, chasing themselves away into the distance.

Down below, the soldiers broke into a dispirited run. Bowie could distinctly hear the scrape of their boots on the rocks. More shots fled after them. Then, down below, the muzzle flashes of Mexican rifles sparked in the darkness and bullets hammered off the rocky ledge in front of Bowie.

Moments later, more firing broke out in the distance as Fallon and the men with him opened up.

By dawn, most of the firing had died out in the valley. There was still a group of the enemy holed up halfway along it, crouched down behind the cover of a cluster of high boulders. Moving his men down into the valley and off the high ledge, Bowie motioned to them to spread out and then move in from both sides, making it impossible for any of the Mexican soldiers to escape. Several of the dead littered the hard, rocky floor of the valley and in the pale half-light of the dawn they looked oddly pathetic and out of place there. Bowie steeled himself against any show of sentiment. These men had declared war on the settlers. They still carried rifles and were still dangerous. None of them showed any indication of wanting to surrender, although they had been called upon to do so more than once.

'Throw down your arms and surrender,' he called loudly. The valley picked up the harsh sound of his voice and threw it from one rearing rocky wall to the other, then back again, bouncing it like an invisible ball until it faded into the distance, no longer capable of being heard.

'Can you hear me?' This time, the echo was longer and lasting and little repetitions of his words flung themselves down on him as he crouched behind one of the rocks, waiting for some reply. It came a few moments later. The vicious, slamming explosion of a rifle; a sound which also possessed an echo, but this time a savage and devastating one. For a moment, Bowie felt a sense of surprise. He had half expected the men pinned down there to throw out their rifles and surrender, knowing by now that they surely had no chance of escape and could not hope to defeat the vastly superior force which faced them, hemming them in on two sides. He jerked his head back and down as the bullet struck the rock in front of his face with a savage force and chips of stone struck the side of his head. He had been watching the place where he knew the men to be hiding and had seen nothing. He was tempted to fire into the shadowy darkness, but some sixth sense kept him motionless.

'Open fire again,' he said suddenly. 'It's clear they don't mean to surrender.'

The brusque rattle of rifle fire sounded loud and soul-destroying in the confined space of the valley. Shrieking and savage, the echoes threw themselves from the rocks and there was the harsh, high-pitched whine of bullets ricocheting off the boulders. Two of the Mexicans suddenly burst out of their hiding place, turned to run away from Bowie, only to find that they had run into the fire from the other direction. Both crumpled up within seconds, dropping to their knees, then falling forward into the rocks. The Mexicans were learning that the settlers were doubly dangerous out here, that this was country of their own choosing, that they were now a force with which to be reckoned. These men they faced were no longer a disorganised rabble, but men who had learned to fight the hard way, who would stop at nothing to gain their ends.

Bowie squinted along the sights of his rifle, waited for a target to show itself. There was a sudden movement behind the rocks and he stiffened instinctively while he waited for the man's head to come up. Instead, something white fluttered on the top of a rifle barrel.

'They're surrenderin',' yelled one of the men. 'They've had enough.'

'Stay down out of sight,' yelled Bowie tightly. 'This could be a trick. They'll shoot you down once you step into the open.'

The man sank down on to his knees again, face tight.

Carefully, Bowie eased himself forward, called loudly: 'Throw out your weapons and come out of there with your hands raised.'

The rifle holding the white flag of surrender remained in sight and a moment later, one of the soldiers, holding it in both hands, stepped out into the open. There was an interval when the sweat trickled along the muscles of Bowie's back and down from his eyebrows into his eyes. He retained his tight-fisted grip on the rifle. Two rifles were pushed over the top of the boulder. Unseen hands thrust them barrel first and Bowie felt his finger tighten around the trigger of his own rifle a little, suspicious of this movement. Then the rifles clattered to the ground and a moment later, more followed.

'All right,' he called. 'Step out into the open and if there is any trick, if one of you stays behind out of sight to open fire on us, every man standing in the open will be shot.' Even as he spoke, men moved out from the boulders. There were a dozen in all, two of them clutching torn shoulders, their blood-stained tunics clinging to their bodies.

Finally, satisfied that this was all of the force still alive, Bowie motioned his men to move forward and collect the weapons that had been tossed away. Then the prisoners were formed up and they began the long trek back into Nacogdoches.

The afternoon was half gone and the heat head had reached its full intensity by the time they reached Nacogdoches. Milam was waiting for them, a sharp, small smile on his face. He nodded to Bowie in welcome, threw a quickly appraising glance at the twelve prisoners, then took the other's arm.

'You got some prisoners then,' he said quietly. 'Excellent. We'll question them later. In the meantime, I'd like to hear what happened.'

Briefly, Bowie related details of the fighting in the valley, how the enemy column had ridden straight into the trap. Milam waited until he had finished before speaking. When he finally did speak, however, his face was serious.

'I thought that once we had defeated this group, we would have a breathing space in which to plan our next move. Unfortunately, events are moving more quickly than anyone could have anticipated.'

'In what way?'

'Santa Anna sent a force of men to San Antonio. We drove him out but there's plenty of evidence that Santa Anna himself is leading an expedition there. Colonel Travis wants as many men as he can get. We don't know how long we have before that expedition is formed and gets to San Antonio. Not long, perhaps. I'm sending as many men as I can afford. At the present time, I think we can be sure that things will remain fairly quiet around Nacogdoches. All of their attention is being directed away from here. But if they do capture San Antonio, there's no doubt they'll come here next.'

'That sounds just like Santa Anna,' murmured Bowie. 'Do you know how many men Travis is likely to have under his command?'

Milam shook his head. 'Hard to say. Possibly only a couple of hundred.'

'And Santa Anna?'

Milam shrugged his shoulders. 'That's even more difficult to estimate. Maybe twice that number.'

'If we start out now, we should reach there before any Mexican force,' Bowie said quietly.

'I hope so. But whatever you do, don't underestimate the Mexicans. So far, we've come off better whenever we've fought them, but sooner or later, we're going to find ourselves facing a force we can't defeat.' The other's tone was serious, his face lined by deep marks, etched around the corners of his mouth and eyes.

The following day, Bowie set out with more than a score of men on the long journey to San Antonio. With them, they took seven wagons carrying supplies, powder and ammunition. The first day out of Nacogdoches was slow. They crossed the creek and then moved on into the desert, with the mesas lifting on either side of them like huge domes of rocks, standing up against the cloudless blue of the sky. They had close on two hundred and fifty miles to cover, across some of the worst land in the state. Once they passed out of that which had been taken over by the settlers some ten years before, they entered virgin territory, home of the Indians and renegades. A quarter of a thousand miles, filled with coyotes and wolves, and men with the habits of both. But there was a force of men waiting for them at San Antonio – men who knew that the showdown would soon come.

They crossed the desert badlands in three days, crossed the Trinity river and drove on to the Brazos. Here the country changed. Although still desolate, the desert itself gave way to scrubland, mesquite and here and there tall belts of timber through which they were forced to hack their way.

On the fourth evening, they camped on a high spread of ground overlooking the Brazos. Here it was a broad river, running low between its banks. The weather had held good and there had been no heavy rain to swell the Brazos and make it difficult to cross.

'Likely you're wondering why we're pushing on to San Antonio like this when it seems unlikely that twenty men can turn the trick against the Mexicans when they arrive to attack the town,' Bowie told the others as they squatted around the fire, drinking the scalding hot coffee and chewing on the slabs of tough beef.

'Seems to me we could have done better to stay at Nacogdoches,' murmured one of the men harshly. He teased the beef with the tip of his knife, chewing it with steel before setting his digestive juices to work on it.

'You know what happens if we don't hold San Antonio?' Bowie asked him, lifting his head and staring straight at the other.

'We fall back on Nacogdoches and fight from there,' replied the other.

'It's not as simple as that. You've all seen what's been happenin' in the past. We've had to fight every inch of the way. We managed to drive the Mexicans out when they came the last time, but this time they're determined to finish us for good. I've talked to a lot of the settlers about taking this country away from Mexico and they've maintained that it can't be done, that we're fools to try to fight against professional soldiers unless we get the Government of the United States behind us.'

'You know what I think,' said the other man seriously. 'I

think that they're right.' And as Bowie looked at him in sudden astonishment, he went on: 'I've ridden this country, clear from San Antonio, north to Nacogdoches and even down as far as the Mexico border. I tell you that without more men, armed men, we don't have a chance of taking this country from Mexico, far less of holding it against them.'

'We've got to stop them at San Antonio,' Bowie said fervently.

'Why?' asked the other tautly. He thrust a piece of beef into his mouth and chewed on it reflectively for a long moment staring into the flames. 'Why go on losing men when it will be only a little while before more Mexicans move in to attack again?'

'Because if we can show 'em that we're here to stay and any attempt to take Tejas away from us by force will be met by force, then they may decide to leave us alone. Once we've declared ourselves to be independent of both Mexico and America, then it's up to us to choose with which country we should join, that is if we decide to join either. It could be that we can make Tejas a free and independent nation.'

Another week on the trail, always heading south and west, over the smoothly-flowing Brabos and then on into the wide, open country beyond, down towards the great Colorado river. Here the water was higher than they had found at the Brazos and they were forced to lash the wagons to tree trunks to float them across, swimming their own mounts in the current.

They pulled into San Antonio five days later, finding an uneasy town. Music came from lighted windows, music and laughter and the shouts of men. But over it all, there lay a sense of uneasiness, of the lull that comes before the storm. Bowie sought out Colonel Travis, in command of the forces in San Antonio.

The other studied him carefully with an appraising glance, then nodded to himself as though satisfied with what he saw. 'We're glad to have you with us, Bowie,' he said softly. 'Any man who can fire a rifle is welcome. We know that Santa Anna will soon be marching against us since we drove out General de Cos. This time, however, I'm not so confident that we can do the same thing.'

7
THE ALAMO

San Antonio was one of the towns which had been set up by the Spaniards when Tejas was part of their territory in the Americas. Their influence was visible everywhere from the chapels and missions, all built in the Spanish style, to the small cantinas and wide streets, often palm-lined. There were very few Mexicans here now. Since the defeat of their forces some time before, most of them had left San Antonio, possibly fearing reprisals against them.

But everywhere that one looked, there were armed men of Colonel Travis's force. The rumours which reached the town were many and varied. Some spoke of a large Mexican force moving up swiftly from the south, with many men and guns. Others claimed that there was very little activity to the south, down in the direction of the Mexico border and that Santa Anna was having difficulty in raising a force to march with him and avenge the defeat of General de Cos. No one knew what to believe although as far as Travis was concerned, it was essential that they should be prepared for the worst.

Gun posts were set up in the town and plans laid for a siege should the need arise. It had long been decided that the most satisfactory place for a final battle would be the mission of the Alamo. As a defensive position it was one of the best and most massively constructed in the whole town, commanding an excellent view over the streets leading up to it. A small force would be able to hold out against an army there in the Colonel's view, although Bowie was not quite as convinced of this as the other and said so on several occasions.

Throughout the whole of February, 1836, the defences of San Antonio were built up in readiness for the Mexican attack, which no one now doubted would come soon. Mexican forces were gathering to the south of the town. Daily, reports came in as to their strength and the number of guns they had with them.

The attack on San Antonio, however, did not begin until February 23rd, when a force estimated at close on four thousand men attacked the town. Within hours, it was apparent that it would be impossible to hold the town itself against such a tremendous weight of men and guns and the entire Texan force was withdrawn into the Alamo mission. Standing as it did within a grove of cottonwood, consisting of a chapel, convent yard, convent and hospital building, and surrounded by a strong wall, it was an ideal defensive position.

The firing had continued around the walls of the mission all afternoon. In the sultry heat, it crackled and hammered with a vicious spite that sent little shivers along Bowie's nerves. When he had ridden into San Antonio some weeks before with the rest of his men, he had not expected to find himself holed up like this, unable to get out, surrounded entirely by the enemy. There were other men here, who thought the same. Dave Crockett, woodsman like himself, seemed ill at ease in this place.

A bullet smashed through the window of the room and sent shards of glass in all directions. Swiftly, Bowie went across the room, stood with his body flattened against the wall, peering out into the wide courtyard. As yet, none of the enemy had succeeded in breaching the walls. They were strong, thickly-built and would stand up to almost anything thrown against them. But sooner or later, the enemy would bring up cannons and it would not be long, once that happened, for them to smash down the walls. Then it would be a fight to the finish and against four thousand men, they had little chance of continuing the struggle for long once the enemy got through the wall.

From where he stood, it was possible to look down over the top of the wall to where the Mexicans were crouched among the cottonwoods. Sighting quickly, Bowie fired at a dark figure that ran from one spot of concealing cover to another. The man staggered as the bullet found its mark, then continued to move forward, dragging one leg behind him. Obviously it had not been a killing shot. Before Bowie could reload and fire again, the other had disappeared.

At the other side of the room, Crockett turned. His face split in a wide grin. Nothing seemed to disturb his unruffled equanimity. 'Better not waste any more bullets like that, Jim,' he said quietly. 'There are too many of them if we do.'

'I wonder if Travis realises how precarious our position is? There's no hope of any force getting through to us in time to save us.'

Crockett nodded. 'They've got forty men for every one of ours and they can bring up fresh supplies of ammunition whenever they like. The only thing we have in our favour is that we don't have to worry about the water supply. We've got more than enough here to last us all the time we'll be needing it.'

Bowie stared at the other in surprise, astonished that the man could take this so calmly. 'Then you feel the same way as I do. That none of us are going to get out of this place alive,' he said seriously.

The other shrugged. 'It isn't going to be easy,' he admitted, in his quiet drawl. 'I don't see any way of slipping through their lines and those walls won't hold for ever. All we can hope to do is take as many of 'em with us as we can.'

Bowie tightened his lips, drew in a deep breath,

surprised at the stab of pain that lanced through his chest. There was a coldness in him which he found hard to explain. His head throbbed oddly and there was a dull, nagging ache at the back of his eyes. With an effort, he forced himself to remain on his feet, peering into the bright sunlight which hurt his eyes, watching for any sign of a fresh attack through the cottonwoods. For the time being, the enemy appeared to have withdrawn some distance from the Alamo, content to bide their time, knowing that they had all the time in the world on their side, whereas it was running out quickly for the defenders of the Alamo.

Several shots came from the other side of the chapel, but they seemed to be utterly remote, and to have nothing to do with him. He rubbed a hand across his forehead, felt the perspiration on his brows, although the room felt oddly cold.

Behind them, Travis came into the room. He seemed to have aged ten years since Bowie had last seen him. Clearly the responsibility of directing this battle was beginning to tell on him. There was a bloody gash across his forehead and blood was oozing slowly from the wound, but he did not seem to be aware of it. He let his gaze travel around the small room, eyeing every man there.

'They seem to have withdrawn for the time being,' he murmured finally. 'But they won't go far. Soon, they'll attack again, hoping to breach the wall.'

'I suppose there's no chance at all of reinforcements getting through to us in time, Colonel,' said one of the men tightly.

'None at all, I'm afraid. We're completely cut off. I suppose you could say that I ought to have seen this coming and made plans to meet such a large force.'

'Seems to me there was nothing you could do about it, Colonel,' said Crockett mildly. 'You only had so many men and pulling back to this mission was the only course left open to you.'

'Thank you.' The other nodded his head ponderously.

Bowie of the Alamo

He sank down into one of the chairs, stretched his legs out in front of him, running a finger along the side of his nose. 'I think we can continue to hold out so long as the wall holds. Once they break through there, it will be only a matter of time before they overrun our position. It will be quite out of the question to try to hold out in any of the buildings for long, either here in the chapel, or in the hospital.'

Through the narrow window, Bowie was able to make out more of the enemy as they began to edge their way forward. So far, they had been unable to make any impression whatever on the wall that ran around the entire mission. He smiled a little to himself, aware of the murmur of voices in the room at his back, but not fastening on to any of them. It was almost as if the voices were reaching him from a tremendous distance, fading and then coming closer in some inexplicable way.

Yes, that priceless, indispensable wall. Without it, the entire command would have been utterly wiped out that very first day when the Mexican force had attacked. It was that wall, thick and high, that kept the enemy, as a body, at a distance. Hour after hour, throughout that long afternoon and into the evening, the fighting continued unabated. Where the enemy got all of their powder and ammunition was a mystery, but shots poured into the defences from every direction, and it seemed the Mexicans had ammunition to waste. The number of enemy slowly increased and many more dropped under the withering and accurate fire of the men manning the wall.

Colonel Travis was an able, energetic, yet cautious man and his responsibility pressed hard on him. Bowie guessed that he had slept little since the assault on the mission had begun. There were deep lines etched in the flesh around his mouth and red circles under his eyes as he came in the following morning shortly after first light to check the defences. His tired gaze watched Bowie closely and a moment later, he came up to him, touched him on the shoulder.

'You hurt at all, Jim?' he asked concernedly.

Bowie shook his head, surprised at the pain which lanced through his neck and shoulders as he did so. Some of it must have shown through on his face for the colonel said tightly. 'Sure you're all right? You look to me as though a good sleep is the one thing you really need right now.'

With an effort, Bowie forced a quick smile. 'If you'll forgive me for saying so, Colonel, I was about to make the same remark myself about you.'

Travis's lips twitched in what might have passed for a smile, but it was impossible to be sure in the pale halflight that filtered through the narrow window into the room. 'The situation worries me,' he confessed softly, his voice carrying only to the man in front of him. 'We've lost several men during the night, and even though it seems we've killed far more of the enemy, it hasn't reduced the tremendous odds against us.'

'You're not thinking of surrendering, sir?' Bowie stared at the Colonel in sudden astonishment.

'I must confess that the thought had crossed my mind, but I rejected it almost immediately. I know that very few of the men under my command would obey that order even if I gave it. But I do wonder what it is that we're fighting for here. If we're all to be destroyed – and judging from the mood Santa Anna is reputed to be in – he'll certainly not rest until every man is dead, will it make any difference on the course of the struggle as a whole?' His voice had dropped very low until now it was little more than a hoarse whisper. His face seemed grey under the tan and Bowie noticed that his hands were trembling a little as he held them in front of him.

'If we can't defeat them, at least we can die fighting like men,' said Bowie harshly. He rubbed a hand over his aching forehead.

'I thought you'd say that,' nodded the other. This time, the smile was very definitely there. Inwardly, Travis was considering what kind of a man this was who stood lean-

Bowie of the Alamo 147

ing against the wall, his rifle beside him, so damned unmilitary in his bearing and yet one of the best men under his command; a man who could barely cipher out his own name, who had never studied military tactics in any formal manner, yet who could sum up the position as adroitly and succinctly as any officer he had ever known.

Then he nodded slowly to himself. This man, like Dave Crockett, had spent all of his life up in the wild untamed lands of the north, had moved with that bunch of men who had pioneered the trails of northern Tejas some years before, a man who could take right good care of himself and any men who fought with him, with or without orders.

Firing broke out on their right. The enemy fire was answered almost at once by defensive fire. For several minutes it continued unabated, then died away as swiftly as it had begun.

'They know they have us licked,' Travis said thickly. 'They can afford to wait and bide their time, knowing that no one can get through to help us in time. We're cut off from all aid and they're well aware of the fact.'

More firing flared up and Travis said sharply. 'We'd better get out to the wall, that sounds like big trouble this time.'

With an effort, Bowie forced himself to his feet, moved out of the chapel and across the open stretch of ground to the wall. Men were already there, crouched in position, firing down on the enemy as they attempted to rush forward. They were under fire before they got to the wall, with bullets striking the ground as they ricocheted off the slabs of stone. Bowie saw one man go down, clutching at his leg. No, he was up again, limping forward, with blood showing on his pants, a wide red stain that was growing slowly wider. With a rush, they made it to the scant protection of the wall. went down behind it, listening to the bullets pecking at the stone like so many birds. Travis was yelling orders in the distance, the lash of his voice reaching them even above the hammering bark of the rifles and the yelling of the enemy.

The man beside Bowie suddenly uttered a harsh, shrill cry. He reeled back from the wall and there was blood on his neck, oozing between his fingers as he put up his hands to it, as if trying to stop the flow. Then he toppled backward, hit the ground hard, like an empty sack and folded up, lying still and unmoving. Chewing on a sour anger, Bowie risked a quick glance, saw the small knot of figures that raced forward, weaving in and out of the trees. Levelling the rifle, he fired and saw one of the running men go down. Without pausing to reload, realising in a sudden flash of intuition that the rest meant to continue forward and not go under cover, he snatched the two pistols from his belt and fired them one after the other. Both bullets found their mark. One man flopped on to his face and lay still. The other slithered forward for several feet, carried onward by the rush of his own momentum. Then his legs gave under him as though unable to bear his weight and going down, he fell over the body of his slain companion. Even though wounded, he snatched at one of the rifles lying on the ground near him, sat up, and tried to level the weapon, bringing it to bear on Bowie.

The man beside Bowie fired, the report deafening in his ears. Out of the corner of his eye, he saw the sitting man suddenly slump sideways as the bullet took him between the eyes, half spinning his body round. This was not an orderly assault. This was a series of sharp attacks, seemingly disconnected, yet all designed to keep the defenders on their toes and to use up their store of ammunition. Somewhere along the wall, a man yelled loud and long, then toppled forward, crashed to the ground on the outside, the impact of his body raising the white dust.

Bowie reloaded mechanically. His mind did not seem to be functioning properly at all. It was as if his hands moved without any real effort of will, as though they were no longer a part of his body. His brain felt strangely empty and hollow.

The enemy were well up now, less than thirty feet from the wall at this point, but now they were forced to expose themselves more and more to the desperate fire of the defenders. More and more went down in their mad, insane rush, in their attempt to breach the wall, to gain a point of entry, through which they could push their overwhelming forces. Bowie crouched low, the harsh stench of the burnt powder in his nose and throat, going down into his lungs until they burned like fire in his aching chest. He sucked in great breaths of air in an effort to relieve the torment in his body, but it did little good. It was difficult to say whether the enemy's numbers had thinned appreciably or not. From back beyond the chapel he heard more rifle fire, guessed that an assault had been launched in that direction too, possibly in an effort to split the defences. He thrust himself forward, keeping his head well down, aware that the men on either side of him were firing slowly and steadily now. Dirt flew in spurts as they fired down on the enemy forcing them back towards the dubious shelter of the trees.

Out on the fleeting edge of vision he saw two of the enemy rise up from the tall grass less than ten feet from the bottom of the wall, where they had lain hidden from view, saw them lift their weapons and try to draw a bead on the men directly above them. Without pausing to think, he lifted himself up to his full height, gripping the pistols in both hands, exposing himself recklessly to the probing enemy fire that rattled along the whole length of the wall at this point. Something stung his left arm, but he was scarcely aware of it. Down below, the rifles spurted flame. A bullet struck the wall close to him and powdered stone hammered against him. Then he fired at the two men, saw the nearer man drop his rifle and reel back, eyes wide and staring in his head, lips twisted into a soundless yell of agony. The other man was hit in the arm. Dropping his weapon, he turned and ran, his legs pumping like pistons over the rough ground. Reaching the nearer fringe of trees, he flung himself wildly forward on to his hands and knees and crawled into the bushes.

In one swift glance, Bowie took in the stretch of ground

just beyond the wall. More than a score of bodies lay there, arms and legs outstretched, some with their faces upturned to the grey dawn light, others face downward in the dirt and grass. One of them was feebly moving, twisting on to its arms and knees, striving to wriggle forward, head lolling drunkenly on its shoulders. From somewhere further along the wall a rifle blasted and the man dropped forward and lay still.

Turning, aware that the firing here had dwindled to only a fraction of what it had been a few moments before, Bowie saw the men near him crouched quiet and still, gripping their smoking rifles, some of them coughing on the smoke and fumes that hung in the still, unmoving air in blue whorls.

The sun came up and the harsh light struck through the curtain of smoke over the wall. The wounded were being lifted from the wall and taken back into the small chapel. It was surprising how few of them there seemed to be. Certainly the Mexican force had suffered far more casualties. But how many more men did they have in San Antonio, men who had not yet been brought into the battle, were being held in reserve until the defenders of the Alamo had been worn down, were unable to continue the battle?

That was the real problem, he thought dully, shaking his head a little. His breathing seemed harsh and stertorous in his throat and every move he made brought pain jarring through his body. He felt the sweat start out on his forehead once more, even though there was, as yet, very little heat in the air, with the sun only just above the horizon. What was wrong with him? he wondered inwardly. He had not been wounded during the fighting, except for the slight nick along his arm where a ricochet had sliced through the skin, tearing the flesh but not touching the bone. Surely that hadn't brought on this feeling of weakness and pain?

Inside the small chapel, he sank down into one of the chairs and tried to force himself to think clearly, but the pounding ache inside his head continued unabated, in spite of everything he could do. He was still sitting there when Travis came into the room. The other saw him instantly and came over, concern on his face.

'You don't look too good to me, Jim,' said the other tightly. 'Are you sure you're all right.' The other glanced down at the stain on Bowie's sleeve, felt his arm and made to draw the material away from the wound, but Bowie shook his head slowly. 'It isn't that, Colonel,' he said harshly. 'It must be something else. A fever, I think. I've felt it coming on for a couple of days now, something I can't throw off no matter how hard I try.'

'I'll get the doctor to take a look at you,' said the other. He spoke in a tone that brooked of no argument, noticing the look in Bowie's eyes as he spoke. 'Just you stay there until he comes in. And I won't hear any more from you about goin' out there and takin' your place an the wall. We still have enough men to man the wall and make sure none of the enemy break through.'

Bowie opened his mouth to protest, then closed it again and allowed himself to sink back into the chair, glad of the fact that he did not have to argue, that the other was giving him the orders now. Travis went out of the room and ten minutes later the tall, thin-faced doctor came in, stood for a moment staring down at him, then reached out for his wrist, feeling the pulse, staring at his eyes.

'Better lie down on one of the beds here and let me make a closer examination,' said the other after a brief pause.

Bowie somehow got to his feet and walked over to one of the empty beds, let himself flop down on it. There was a terrible weakness in his body now and his legs seemed to have turned to water, unable to hold him. The throbbing ache in his head, at the back of his eyes, seemed to have grown in intensity until it pounded away in his brain, bringing an actual pain to his head.

The doctor pulled off his shirt, then tapped his chest in several places with his fingertips, his face serious. But it was difficult to read anything into that expression. Finally, the other seemed satisfied. He motioned to Bowie to slip his shirt on again, but he did not tell him to sit up.

'I'm afraid it looks to me as though you have pneumonia,' he said quietly, his voice soft. 'I may be wrong, but I think it would be wise for you to remain here for a few days anyway.'

'But I can't stay in bed,' protested Bowie vehemently. 'Not while the others are being killed defending this place. You know as well as I do that the Colonel needs every man who can handle a rifle.'

'But not a man in your condition,' persisted the other. He placed his hand on Bowie's chest as the other made to push himself up on to his elbows and thrust him down again with a surprising strength. 'Now lie still. If you do exactly as I tell you and stay in bed, you may be up and about in a few days.'

Bowie smiled grimly and mirthlessly. 'Don't you realise that we may all be dead within a few days, Doctor,' he said tersely.

'Maybe so. But that doesn't alter the fact that you're seriously ill and you could certainly not handle a rifle. At the moment, you are no use whatever to the colonel and the sooner you accept that fact, the better it will be for you, and the easier for me.'

The other rose to his feet, stood for a long moment beside the bed, staring down at Bowie. Then he said quietly. 'I understand how you feel, Mister Bowie. You want to be out there with the others, defending this place. But at the moment, that is quite out of the question. I ought to warn you that unless you do as I say, you'll be dead within the next two days, and not from a bullet.'

Turning on his heel, he stalked out of the room. Lying flat on the long bed, Bowie stared up at the low ceiling, dimly aware of the sound of firing and shouting it in the distance. His head ached and his chest felt as if it were on fire. For a long moment, he continued to stare into space, trying to think clearly, to get ideas straight in his mind and finding it difficult to do so. His thinking seemed to be oddly muddled and thoughts kept spinning around inside his mind, aimlessly and chaotically. Finally, he fell asleep, only vaguely aware that someone had entered the room. There had been the momentary impression of a man coming forward to the bed and looking down at him as if from a tremendous distance and then the darkness came and he seemed to be falling forward for countless leagues into a deep and totally dark abyss.

He was awake and aware that he was awake, although the room was in darkness and beyond the windows there was only the blackness of night. For several minutes, he lay quite still, shivering one moment, burning with fever the next. He could hear no sound and it came to him that perhaps the fighting was over, that somehow, by some strange miracle, the enemy had been beaten off, or help had got through to them in time. Then he let his mind wander a little in his head. Flashes of memory brought back scenes to his mind from long ago. He recalled the time he had sat with Collie Thorpe and McGee in the lee of the tall hill, waiting for the night to come and with it Lafitte's ship from the Bay, bringing with it the Negro slaves they would take into New Orleans.

Then, abruptly, his mind switched and another scene formed clearly. The great stretching swamp on the far bank of the Mississippi, over from New Orleans, where he had spent all of those long months with Lafitte, while Thorpe and McGee had gone off on their own to seek the rich travellers moving along the trails to the west. The scene in his mind's eye was so real and lifelike that he could almost smell that sweet, sometimes sickly, stench of vegetation rotting in the ooze and hear the faint slap of the muddy water against the tree roots of the Bayou.

With an effort, he pushed himself upright, remained like that for a moment, as the blood rushed pounding painfully to his temples and the room swayed in the darkness around him. He felt weak and light-headed and he was aware of his heart thumping madly against his ribs as he sucked air down into his lungs. Finally, the pain in his head was so great that he was forced to lie back on the hard pillow and close his eyes. Gradually, the heaving in his chest stilled and his heart slowed into a more normal beat. The sweat had boiled out on his body and his shirt clung to him. Carefully, he rolled his head to his right and stared in the direction of the nearby window. He could just make out the square of darkness that was the patch of night sky which lay beyond it. A bright star had eased its way into one corner of that square and he found that by shifting his gaze a little, he could see more, much fainter spots of light, close beside the solitary bright one. He let his breath go in a long, pent-up sigh. What was happening out there at that moment? he wondered tautly. Were the enemy creeping up on to the defences, ready to take them completely by surprise, to rush the wall and break down their only line of defence, surging into the mission and slaughtering every man inside? The thought grew stronger in his mind as he lay there, straining his ears to pick up the faintest sound. More and more, the conviction grew in him that the defenders who were supposed to be out there at that moment, keeping watch for the enemy, were asleep at their posts. Unable to prevent himself, he uttered a wild, loud cry, that echoed through the room.

Desperately, he tried to swing his legs to the cold floor of the room, to get to his feet, but his legs were unable to hold him. He swayed and would have fallen forward on to his face had not strong hands seized him from behind, easing him gently back on to the bed, stretching his body under the sheets.

'Better lie still,' said a voice close to his ear.

'But the enemy! They're—' His voice trailed away into silence as the other murmured quietly.

'They won't attack tonight. We drove them off shortly before midnight. They'll need time to regroup their forces before they come in again. Now just you lie still and I'll get the doctor for you.'

Bowie lay back on the cool pillow, lips pressed tightly together. The odd stillness still pervaded the entire mission. It was as though the entire world hung trembling on the brink of a deep, black abyss of silence, not wanting to make a single sound. Then there was movement in the doorway and the tall figure of the doctor came striding in. He had thrown on his coat over his night attire and his face was lined with weariness.

'I found him trying to get to the window,' said the man who had come to help him. 'He seemed to be out of his head. Yelling something about the enemy getting through the defences, that he had to go and help them.'

'Delirious,' said the doctor tautly. 'I'll give him a sleeping draught. It should keep him asleep until well into tomorrow morning. By then, the fever may have left him.'

'Do you think he'll be all right, Doctor?' asked the man, standing in the shadows behind the bed.

'I think so. He's got one of the strongest constitutions I've ever come across and he's spent most of his life outdoors, which goes a long way in a case such as this.' More grimly, the other went on: 'What worries me so much is that I may be only saving him from this, to deliver him into the hands of the Mexicans. There isn't any doubt in my mind what our fate is going to be once they succeed in breaking down the wall and getting inside the mission.'

He got to his feet, moved out of the room, only to come back a few moments later with something in a glass, something he held out to Bowie's lips, holding his head so that he might get the bitter-tasting liquid down. For a moment, he almost choked on it, but somehow he managed to get it down and keep it down. The other sat on the edge of the low bed until he finally fell asleep then motioned to the man standing in the shadows. Together, they moved noiselessly out of the room. Less than an hour later, firing broke out around the defensive perimeter of the Alamo, but Bowie heard nothing of it. In the drug-induced sleep, he lay oblivious of all that went on around him.

Slowly, the fever left him, but the general weakness remained. He found it still impossible to remain on his feet for any length of time and although he attempted to maintain that he was fit enough to help the others, the doctor adamantly refused to let him leave his bed.

When Travis came in to see him on the tenth day of the siege, he tried to get the Colonel to overrule the doctor's orders, but the other merely shook his head and said quietly. 'You'd be killed before you could even lift a rifle.' The other's head swung towards him. 'In a day or so, you ought to be able to get up from your bed and by that time, we'll be glad to have you back with us. In the meantime—'

'In the meantime, I'm just a hindrance to everybody. Is that it?'

'Now you know that ain't true, Jim,' persisted the other loudly. 'But I can't have a sick man with my men. I'd have enough time cut out looking after them, without having to keep a sharp eye on you.'

Bowie lay quiet, trying to hold on to what he heard. The other's voice seemed to keep on drifting away, as if he were speaking more and more softly. Then it would strengthen and burgeon up again, ringing in his ears.

'How many men do we have left?' He wished he could get more strength and power into his voice, but it seemed to come from somewhere deep in his chest and lost a lot of its old timbre and resonance on the way out through his mouth.

'We still have plenty to hold 'em off with,' affirmed the other heartily. But Bowie could see the haunted look at the back of the colonel's eyes and knew that what he said was far from the truth. By now, the situation would be pretty serious and the enemy's strength had probably been increased in readiness for one last big assault on the mission. If only he had the strength to get to his feet and stay on them without this feeling of falling and dizziness that came every time he attempted to lift his head.

'You're not even a very good liar, Colonel,' he said weakly, with a faint smile on his lips. 'But you're right. I still don't feel as though I could get to my feet and stay there. God, what's the matter with me? When I should be out there with the others, I'm lyin' here like some child, unable to do anythin'.'

'You've been ill,' said the other quietly. 'The doctor reckons that any lesser man would have died with this disease. Only your constitution pulled you through the crisis. Even then, we didn't think you were goin' to make it.'

Bowie tried to move, disregarding the darting daggers of pain in his body. He was glad that he seemed to be able to think more clearly than before. Thoughts were not so fuzzy in his mind and there were no longer those extremely vivid pictures of his past to bother him.

A hand reached out and forced him to lie still. 'Easy now,' said the colonel. 'We don't want to undo all of the good work that the doctor has put in over the past few days. Besides, he's got plenty on his hands at the moment, coping with the wounded. You'll be all right if you just lie still now and let nature do her work to finish healing you.'

The effort to push himself up had drained almost all of the strength and feeling from his body and Bowie lay back on the pillow, utterly spent, lying quiet after the other had gone away, his mind drifting in and out of the deeper darkness of unconsciousness which was still very close to him. At intervals he awoke to hear the unmistakable sounds of heavy firing and yelling in the distance and some of the old fire would come back into his veins and he longed to be on his feet once more, joining with the others, to feel the cold steel of a rifle or his faithful knife under his fingers.

But these intervals passed, there were moments of sleep and moments when more voices made a deep and senseless clamour in his brain, beating at him sharp and curiously irritating, meaningless, mingled with the sharp bark of shots, pounding through his mind. Something at the back of his brain told him that the enemy had not once ceased their attack on the Alamo, that they were now striving to break through the wall which was their only defence, that once they succeeded, it would all be over for the men inside the mission, that the Mexicans would have retaken San Antonio and then they might head for Nacogdoches, striving to throw out the Americans there. But whether they did so or not, would not matter in the slightest to any of the defenders of the Alamo. They would all have been dead and possibly forgotten by then. They would have given all they had for this cause, for the freedom of the American settlers in Tejas.

With a tremendous effort, he forced himself up on to his elbows and stared about him. His pistols were close at hand, loaded, ready for use. Under his pillow, his groping fingers encountered the hard, smooth steel of his knife. He pulled it out into the faint light, staring down at it, running his tongue around his caked, cracked lips.

Outside, beyond the window of his room, he heard the sudden savage yell, felt his heart leap within him, although he did not know why. Something had happened out there, he felt sure of that, and the knowledge made him drop the knife on to the sheet and reach out to grip the pistols, holding them tightly in both hands. There was the unmistakable sound of running feet, a confused yelling in the courtyard, boots clattering on the steps and the harsh, triumphant shouts of men. A rifle banged in the yard outside the building. Someone yelled an order in Mexican and he knew with a sick certainty that the wall had been breached, that the enemy had finally forced their way into the mission.

How long he lay there, waiting, staring at the door in front of him, it was impossible to tell. Time held no meaning for him now. There was a dull ache at the back of his eyes but he was almost glad of it now. Certainly, he scarcely felt it. Something was welling up inside his mind, something he had felt on only one or two occasions in the past; the feeling of coming achievement, of knowing just why he was there and what he had to do.

There was a sudden commotion outside the door, a

hammering on the wood. Then it burst open and a group of Mexican soldiers came pushing into the room. One of them saw him on the bed, uttered a loud yell, ran forward and died instantly as one of the pistols in Bowie's hands went off with a roar and a flash of light. The dead man had scarcely hit the floor before the others moved forward. Bowie glimpsed their faces, had but a confused impression of them coming towards him. He fired the other pistol, felt it jerk in his hand and saw the nearest man stagger back with blood pouring from the wound in his throat. He screamed and went down out of sight.

Both pistols were now useless. As the men came on, Bowie hurled first one and then the other at his assailants. One of the guns caught a swarthy featured man just below the right eye and the foresight tore the flesh away, sending blood trickling down his cheek.

Snatching up the knife, he heaved himself up on to the bed. There was a new strength in his body now, a feeling of savage exultation. Gone was the weakness that had plagued him for the past ten days. He slashed at the nearest man, felt the blade of the knife find its mark. Blood spurted over his hand. The man uttered a shrill bleat of pain and staggered back, clutching at his stomach.

Something struck a burning furrow along his side and there was the thunderous report of a rifle going off close to him in the room. He scarcely felt the pain in his body, was merely aware of the warm blood flowing down his side. More men came running into the room. The thought flitted across his mind that it took more than a dozen Mexicans to kill one American. Then something struck him hard on the side of the head. He tried to lash out with the knife, but his arm refused to obey his will. There was a darkness hovering in front of his vision and it was getting more and more difficult to see what was going on around him. Faces kept wavering and blurring in front of his eyes. He struck out feebly, but felt nothing and there was a harsh, triumphant shout roaring in his ears.

Then another shot rang out, but he hardly heard it.

The shot had torn into his vital parts but although there was a sense of shock, there was no feeling of pain. A sudden deluge of bright red filmed his vision and now he could no longer see anything. With the deluge came a quick warmth accompanied by a faintly pleasant sensation, as if he were no longer lying on the hard bed, but were floating above it, his body light, with all of the pain and weakness washed away. He felt his head go forward and for a brief moment there was a protesting pain in his body, then the red faded into purple and black and there was nothing at all . . .

Of the men who had defended the Alamo, there were only five survivors, and these were slaughtered in cold blood on Santa Anna's orders. They had taken more than five hundred of the enemy with them during their desperate struggle and their struggle had not been in vain. Less than seven weeks later, Santa Anna was defeated and captured by the Texans under Sam Houston at San Jacinto.